W9-BYN-994

DN 10-10

pink

WANDA &
BRUNSTETTER

Betsy's
RETURN

BRIDES *of* LEHIGH CANAL

BOOK TWO

BARBOUR
PUBLISHING

For more information about Wanda E. Brunstetter, please access the author's Web site at the following Internet address: www.wandabrunstetter.com

Cover design: Faceout Studio, www.faceoutstudio.com
Cover photo: Pixelworks Studios, www.shootpw.com

Published by Barbour Publishing, Inc., P.O. Box 719, Uhrichsville, OH 44683, www.barbourbooks.com.

Our mission is to publish and distribute inspirational products offering exceptional value and biblical encouragement to the masses.

ecpa Member of the
Evangelical Christian
Publishers Association

Printed in the United States of America.

DEDICATION/ACKNOWLEDGMENTS

To my husband, who's also my pastor,
and to pastors everywhere who give so much of themselves
in order to minister to the needs of their congregations.

Chapter 1

Summer 1896

"Oh, Papa, I'm so sorry." Betsy Nelson dabbed at her tears and sank to the bed in the small room she occupied in New York City. She had just received a telegram saying that her father had suffered a heart attack and would have to resign his position as pastor of the community church in Walnutport, Pennsylvania.

"It isn't fair," Betsy moaned, as she let her mind take her back to the days when Papa, newly widowed, had begun his ministry at the small church not far from the Lehigh Canal. Betsy had been a young girl then, barely out of pigtails. Grieving over her mother's untimely death, she had been an angry, disagreeable child, often saying spiteful things so others would feel as badly as she did. Even as an adult she had made cutting remarks and looked down her nose at those she thought were beneath her.

She remembered when she had tried to get Mike Cooper's attention. Besides being young, handsome, and single, Mike ran a general store along the Lehigh Canal. There'd been one problem—Mike was interested in Kelly McGregor, an unkempt young woman who led the mules that pulled her father's canal boat.

Betsy grimaced at the memory of the harsh words that had come from her mouth the day she'd invited herself to join Mike and Kelly on a picnic. They'd been talking about swimming, and Mike had admitted that he'd never learned to swim well. Betsy had turned to Kelly and asked, "What about you? As dirty as you get trudging up and down the dusty towpath, I imagine you must jump into the canal quite frequently in order to get cleaned off."

Five years later Betsy could still picture Kelly's wounded expression and see the look of horror on Mike's face.

"They must have thought I was terrible. I'm surprised the board of deacons didn't fire Papa because of me," she murmured. Yet despite Betsy's curt, self-righteous ways, the church leaders had remained patient with her, just as her dear father had.

Betsy closed her eyes, and a vision of Papa standing behind the pulpit came to mind. In his younger days he'd been a handsome man with curly, dark hair and gray blue eyes that reflected the concern and compassion he felt for others. He'd preached strong sermons from the Bible and played the fiddle with enthusiasm, and despite his disagreeable daughter, everyone in the congregation respected and admired the Reverend Hiram Nelson.

Betsy squeezed her fingers around the telegram, crumpling it into a tight ball and letting it fall to the floor. "It's not right that Papa should have to give up something he's done for so many years. If only his heart had remained strong. If only God would give us a miracle."

She stood and moved over to the window, staring at the street below. An ice wagon rolled past, probably heading to one of the nearby stores to make a delivery. Several horses plodded down the street, pulling various-sized buggies transporting businessmen to their office jobs. A newspaper boy stood on one corner, heralding the news of the day. A peddler selling his wares ambled down the road, pushing his cart full of pots and pans. New York City was always busy, even in these early morning hours.

Betsy leaned against the window casing and thought about how much her life had changed over the last four years. She'd left Walnutport in 1892, and soon after her arrival in New York City, where she was to meet with the mission board, she had been beaten and robbed. A gentle, caring woman named Abigail Smith, an officer in the Salvation Army, had taken Betsy into her home and nursed her back to health. By the time Betsy's wounds had healed, she knew the

Salvation Army was a worthy cause and she wanted a part in it. Since that time she'd found a closer relationship with Christ and had joined others from the Salvation Army in numerous street meetings, often playing her zither, singing, and proclaiming the Word of God to anyone who would listen. She'd also spent many hours at the Cheap Food and Shelter Depot, which helped the poor and downtrodden obtain a new lease on life.

Betsy's ties with the Salvation Army had also presented her with an opportunity to volunteer at a local orphanage. She, who had previously been uncomfortable around children, now found pleasure in working with underprivileged orphans so in need of love and attention. For the first time in Betsy's thirty-one years she found herself wishing she had children of her own. She supposed some women were destined to be old maids, and she was convinced that she would be one of them.

Betsy's mind snapped back to the present situation with her father's ill health and his resignation from the church. A new preacher would soon be assigned to take Papa's place, and that didn't feel right to Betsy. Neither did Papa being sick.

A spark of anger ignited a flare of determination in her heart as she moved away from the window and knelt in front of the trunk at the foot of her bed. "I must set my work in New York City aside and return home. Papa needs me to care for him now."

Dear William Covington:

*The board of deacons from the Walnutport
Community Church in Pennsylvania would like to
interview you, for our previous pastor, the Rev. Hiram
Nelson, recently suffered a heart attack and has been
forced to retire. If you're willing to meet with us, please
notify me as soon as possible.*

Sincerely,

Ben Hanson

Head Deacon

William folded the letter he'd received yesterday and placed it on the rolltop desk sitting in the far corner of his father's study. It had only taken him a few hours to deliberate before he'd sent a telegram to Deacon Hanson, letting him know that he would arrive at the train depot in Easton, Pennsylvania, on Friday and would rent a carriage to make the trip to Walnutport. That would give him the opportunity to meet with the board of deacons on Saturday, as well as tour the church and parsonage. On Sunday he would meet the members of his prospective congregation and give them a sample of his preaching.

William strolled back across the room and took a seat on the elegant sofa his mother had purchased on her recent trip to England. He leaned back, stretching his arms overhead, and yawned. He was glad for this opportunity to be alone with his thoughts. His parents had gone to the opera tonight, and even though William's mother had tried to convince him to go along, he had politely declined, saying he needed time to pack for the trip and prepare his sermon.

William's gaze came to rest on the massive portrait of his father, hanging on the far wall. William Covington Jr. had been born into a wealthy family and had inherited all his father's business ventures after William Sr. died several years ago. William III had no desire to follow in his father's or grandfather's footsteps as a successful entrepreneur. The fact that William's father owned a thriving newspaper in Buffalo, New York, as well as several hotels, the new music hall, and numerous specialty stores, meant nothing to William. He had accepted Christ as his Savior when he was twelve years old, and ever since then, his strongest desire had been to become a minister. Three and a half months ago he'd graduated from the seminary in Boston, full of hope for the future and anxious to marry Beatrice Lockhart, his high school sweetheart.

William groaned as a vision of Beatrice came to mind—ebony hair and eyes the color of dark chocolate. Soon after they'd begun courting, Beatrice had agreed to marry him. The wedding had been set for the week after William graduated from seminary, and his future bride had seemed excited about the idea of being the wife of a "prominent minister," as she liked to refer to William whenever they were with her friends. But when William had informed Beatrice that his first church might be small and unable to pay him much money, she'd insisted that he give up the idea of becoming a preacher and go to work for his father. Certain that God had called him to the ministry, William had refused her request. Beatrice pouted at first, the way she'd always done whenever she didn't get her way. Then she'd finally given in and said she would abide by whatever William decided.

"She lied to me!" William shuddered at the memory of standing at the altar, waiting for a bride who never showed up. A note had been delivered by Beatrice's father. Beatrice had changed her mind; she didn't want to be a minister's wife after all. *"Too many demands,"* she'd written. *"It might take years before you're hired at a church that would be able to support us adequately."*

William folded his arms and leaned forward, a deep groan escaping his lips. He could never trust another woman or get over the humiliation of being jilted by Beatrice. He'd thought she loved him for better or worse, richer or poorer, but he'd been sorely mistaken.

He stood, prepared to return to the desk and work on the sermon he would deliver to the people in Walnutport, but raucous yapping distracted him. His mother's Siamese cat raced into the room, with his father's English setter nipping at her tail. The dog had obviously sneaked into the house, probably because William had left the door ajar when he'd gone out for some fresh air after his parents left. Thanks to his carelessness, muddy paw prints now covered Mother's Persian rug.

"Lucius, come here!"

The dog ignored William and kept chasing the hissing, spitting cat.

William quickly joined the chase, hoping to capture his father's prized hunting dog and remove him from the house. But each time Lucius was within William's grasp, the animal eluded him. In the meantime, Princess, the pampered feline, hopped onto a small table, and Lucius leaped into the air and swiped at Princess with his large, muddy paw. The cat jumped to the floor, eluding the setter, but Mother's Parisian vase crashed to the floor.

"I'll never hear the end of this," William groaned. When his mother saw the mess, she would tell him that it would never have happened if he had gone to the opera as they had asked.

William looked up. "Oh Lord, I pray the church in Walnutport accepts me as its pastor, because I need to get away—away from Father's unreasonable demands, from Mother's persnickety ways, and from the memory of the woman who left me standing at the altar."

Chapter 2

As Betsy stepped through the front doorway of the parsonage, a feeling of nostalgia swept over her like a cool wind on a hot summer's day. She had spent the better part of fifteen years in this home, and she and her father had created enough memories to fill up a lifetime.

"Papa, I'm home!" she called.

"I–I'm in the sitting room" came his feeble reply.

Betsy placed her suitcase beside the umbrella stand and rushed into the next room. The sight made her halt in midstride. Her father reclined on the sofa, his face pale and drawn, his hair, once full and shiny, now dull and thinning. He offered a weak smile and pulled himself to a sitting position. "Betsy, it's so good to see you."

She hurried across the room and dropped to her knees in front of the sofa. "Oh, Papa, it's good to see you, too. If I'd known how things were with your health, I would have come much sooner."

He reached out and wiped the moisture from her cheeks with his thumb. "Don't waste your tears on me, daughter. I'm in God's hands, and He will see me through to the end."

The end? Did Papa believe he was dying? Could Papa's heart be so weak that he might not live much longer?

Betsy reached for her father's hand and was saddened by the lack of strength in his grip. Papa used to be so energetic; now he was a mere shell of a man.

"I wish you hadn't felt the need to come home," he said. "Your work with the Salvation Army is important, and people check on me regularly."

Betsy gently massaged his bony fingers. "I'm needed here right now. It's my place to care for you."

Tears welled in Papa's eyes. "You're a good daughter, and I'm much obliged."

Late-afternoon shadows bounced off the walls as Betsy glanced around the room, noting the thick coating of dust on the end tables and fireplace mantle. "Is there anything I can get for you, or would you rather I do some cleaning?"

He shook his head, easing himself back to the sofa pillows. "You're probably tired from your train trip, and the cleaning can wait. Why don't you sit awhile so we can visit?"

Betsy rose from her knees. "All right, but first let me fix you a cup of tea."

"That would be nice."

"What kind would you like, herbal or black?"

"A couple of ladies from church came by yesterday and brought some things for the pantry. So whatever you come up with is fine."

"I'll be back soon." Betsy leaned over and kissed his forehead then hurried to the kitchen. A knock sounded at the back door. When she opened it, she was greeted by two of the church deacons, Ben Hanson and Henry Simms.

"Afternoon, Betsy," Ben said with a nod. "We heard you were coming and thought we'd better get over here and explain things to you."

Betsy opened the door wider, bidding them enter. "Your telegram said my father had a heart attack and that his health has failed so much that he must resign as pastor."

"That's right," Henry said, combing his stubby fingers through his thinning hair. "A minister's on his way here from Buffalo, New York, to interview for the position."

Betsy clenched her teeth. It grieved her to hear them speak of hiring someone to take Papa's place. Yet it wasn't their fault Papa's health had failed. Even though it had been the board of deacons' decision to ask for her father's resignation, the board had had no choice. If Papa could no longer fulfill his duties, it was time for him to step aside.

Ben cleared his throat and shuffled his feet. "The

thing is, once we've hired a new preacher and he moves to Walnutport, he's going to need a place to live."

Henry nodded in agreement. "Since the parsonage was built by the founding church members and is owned by the church, I'm afraid we'll have to ask you and your father to move."

Betsy stood still as she let the deacons' words register. Her father would not be preaching in Walnutport anymore. A minister was coming for an interview. She and Papa would have to look for another place to live.

"You won't have to move until we've hired a new preacher and he's able to relocate." Ben gave the end of his handlebar mustache a quick flick. "It could take several months to find the right man for the job."

"That's right," Henry put in. "I–I'm sure it won't be easy to fill your pa's shoes."

Betsy bit her lip so hard she tasted blood. "Is that all you gentlemen wanted?"

"Yes, yes. I believe we've said all that needs to be said. Give the good preacher our regards!" Ben called over his shoulder as he and Henry hurried out the door.

"I'll do that." Betsy closed the door behind them and headed for the pantry. She found several glass jars filled with vegetables and fruit, a jar of coffee, and a bag of flour on the floor, but no tea.

She released a sigh. "Looks like I'll need to make a trip to Cooper's store and see about getting some tea and a few other things we'll need," she mumbled. "I'd better tell Papa where I'm going."

When she entered the sitting room, she found her father asleep, so she scrawled him a note and left it on the low table in front of the sofa. She didn't think it would take long to get the things she needed, and she'd probably be back long before Papa woke up.

———❖———

As William guided the horse pulling his rented carriage down the dusty road toward Walnutport, he thought about his mother's predictable reaction when he'd told her that he was interviewing to be pastor in a small town near the Lehigh Canal in Pennsylvania.

"Why can't you wait until a church opens here in Buffalo?" she had questioned. "Why would you want to minister to a bunch of country folks?"

"Don't you think I'll be a good enough preacher to shepherd the flock?" William had asked.

"That's not what I meant at all," she had said in a defensive tone.

"What your mother is trying to say is that a small church in the middle of nowhere won't be able to pay you much because there won't be enough people," his father had interjected, giving his goatee a couple of quick pulls.

William gripped the reins tighter. "I shouldn't have

expected them to understand. All Mother cares about is her socialite friends, and all Father worries about is his money."

He drew in a quick breath and blew it out with a huff. "It would have been nice if one of them had been supportive about me going to Walnutport for this interview."

William rounded a bend and spotted a store near the canal, so he decided to stop and get himself something cold to drink. It wouldn't do for the prospective pastor to show up in Walnutport hot, sweaty, and feeling as out of sorts as a dog with a tick on his backside. Maybe a bottle of sarsaparilla was what he needed.

"It's so nice to see you again," Kelly Cooper said, as she wrote up Betsy's purchases. "It's a shame you had to come home under such gloomy conditions though."

Betsy lifted her shoulders and let them drop with a sigh. There was no point giving in to her emotions, for it wouldn't change a thing.

"If there's anything we can do to help, be sure to let us know," Kelly's husband, Mike, offered as he joined his wife behind the counter.

"I appreciate that." Betsy hoped her smile didn't appear forced. She appreciated their concern, but it was hard to think about Papa leaving the ministry, much less to see the pity on Mike's face when he offered support. "What Papa and I need most is your prayers."

"You've sure got those," Kelly said.

Mike nodded his agreement.

"If you hear of anywhere we can move once we're ousted from the parsonage, be sure to let us know."

"I'll keep my eyes and ears opened—you can be sure of that," Mike said.

"Thanks." Betsy was pleased she had developed a pleasant relationship with the Coopers over the years in spite of the way she'd behaved before Mike and Kelly had gotten married. *I'll never throw myself at another man the way I did at Mike,* she determined. *It would be better to remain an old maid for the rest of my life than to embarrass myself like that.*

She glanced around the room. "Where are your two little ones, Kelly?"

"They're over at my sister Sarah's, playing with her kids."

The bell above the front door jingled, and Betsy turned her head. A young man with neatly combed, chestnut-colored hair and the bluest eyes she had ever seen stepped into the store. He wore a dark brown suit and a pair of leather shoes that looked as out of place in Cooper's General Store as a fish trying to make his home on dry land.

"Can I help you, sir?" Mike asked, stepping quickly around the counter.

The man nodded. "I'd like a bottle of sarsaparilla, if you have some."

"Sure do. If you'll wait here, I'll get one from the ice chest."

"I'll do that." The man seemed a bit uncomfortable as he shifted his weight from one foot to the other.

Betsy offered him the briefest of smiles then quickly averted her gaze to the food Kelly was packaging for her.

"I don't recollect seein' you around before," Kelly said, nodding at the man. "Are you visiting someone in the area or just passing through?"

"My name is William Covington, and I've come from Buffalo, New York. I'll be meeting with the board of deacons at the Walnutport Community Church tomorrow about the possibility of becoming their new minister."

Betsy's mouth dropped open, and Kelly glanced her way with a shrug. Betsy had known the board would be interviewing a minister from Buffalo; she just didn't think he would be so young—or so handsome.

Chapter 3

———◆✳◆———

Can you tell me how much farther it is to Walnutport?"
William asked, directing his question to the young woman
who stood behind the counter, with long, dark hair hanging
down her back.

"It's a short drive from here." She nodded toward the
other woman, whose ash-blond hair was worn in a tight bun
at the back of her head. "This is Betsy Nelson, the preacher's
daughter. She could probably show you the way to town."

"You're. . .Rev. Nelson's daughter?"

She nodded. "My father's the man you'll be replacing if
the board of deacons hires you."

William swallowed. "I–I'm sorry about your father's health

problems, and if you would feel awkward about showing me the way to Walnutport, I'll certainly understand."

Miss Nelson lifted her package into her arms. "It would be no bother. I'm going there anyway, and it's not your fault my father has been asked to resign."

William winced, feeling as though he'd been slapped. It might not be his fault Rev. Nelson had been asked to step down from the pulpit, but he was the one who might be taking the poor man's place.

"Here's your sarsaparilla," the young man who ran the store said, handing the bottle to William.

"How much do I owe you?"

The man flashed William a friendly grin. "It's free. Consider it my welcome to our community."

William was tempted to say that he hadn't been hired as the new minister yet and might not be moving to Walnutport, but he took the sarsaparilla gratefully and expressed his thanks.

"I'm ready to head out if you are," Miss Nelson said, nodding toward the front door.

"Yes, I suppose we should." William extended his hand toward the storekeeper. "It was nice to meet you. I'll be preaching at the community church on Sunday, so maybe I'll see you there."

The storekeeper nodded as he shook William's hand. "My name's Mike Cooper, and my wife, Kelly, and I, as well as our two children, attend regularly. We'll look forward to seeing you on Sunday morning."

William smiled. "Good day then." He held the door for Miss Nelson and followed her to a dilapidated buckboard. If the town's minister couldn't afford to drive anything better than this, the church probably didn't pay its pastor much at all.

But I won't be coming here for the money, he reminded himself. *This is my chance to make a fresh start and serve God's people.*

Miss Nelson leaned into the wagon and placed her package on the floor behind the seat. Lifting her long, brown skirt, she started to step up. William was quick to offer his hand, but she shook her head and mumbled, "I've been climbing into this old wagon since I was a girl in pigtails."

William shrugged and headed for his carriage. By the time he'd gathered the reins, Miss Nelson was already heading down the road at a pretty good clip.

"She's either in a hurry, or she has made up her mind that she doesn't like me," he mumbled.

I shouldn't have been so rude to Rev. Covington, Betsy reprimanded herself as she headed down the dusty road toward Walnutport. *I'll need to apologize as soon as we get to town.* She glanced over her shoulder and pulled slightly back on the reins to slow the horse. The reverend's buggy was way behind, and if she didn't allow him to catch up, he might think she didn't want to show him the way to town.

As Betsy continued to travel, she thought about her father. Had he awakened in her absence and found the note she'd left him? Should she tell Papa about the new minister who'd come to interview for his position? Maybe it would be better not to say anything. The interview might not go well, and then the Rev. William Covington would be on his way back to Buffalo, leaving the board of deacons to begin the process of finding another prospective minister.

"Whoa! Whoa! Hold up there, boy!"

Betsy turned in her seat to see what was going on in the minister's rig and was surprised to discover that he'd stopped the horse and was climbing out of his carriage. She halted her horse, stepped down from the buckboard, and walked back to where he stood, holding up his horse's right front foot.

"Is there a problem?"

He nodded. "My horse has thrown a shoe and seems to have picked up a stone. I'm afraid if I keep going along this road he might turn up lame."

Betsy's forehead wrinkled as she mulled over her options. She could leave the reverend here with his rig while she headed for town to see about getting the blacksmith to come shoe the horse, or she could suggest that Rev. Covington tie the horse to a tree, push his carriage off the road, and ride with her. When she got to town, she would drop him off at the blacksmith's shop and let the smithy take things from there. The second option seemed like the polite thing to do, so she suggested it.

"Yes, yes. I suppose it would be wise." He pushed a wayward strand of thick hair off his damp forehead. "If you're sure you don't mind."

"I wouldn't have suggested it if I'd minded." Betsy could have bit her tongue. She was being rude again. "I'm sorry for snapping," she apologized. "And I'm sorry if I sounded curt with you back at the store." She released a sigh. "I'm concerned about my father, and I'm afraid my fears have caused my tongue to be sharper than usual."

"Apology accepted. I understand this must be a difficult time for you and your father," Rev. Covington said, as he unhitched his horse and led him to the closest tree.

"Yes it is," Betsy agreed. "When I got the telegram saying my father had suffered a heart attack and had been forced to retire from the ministry, I knew I should leave my job in New York City and return to Walnutport in order to care for him."

"You were working in New York?"

She nodded. "For the Salvation Army. I've been with them the past four years."

"I see." He tied the horse and moved back to his buggy, which he pushed off the road with little effort.

No questions or comments about the Salvation Army? Was a quick "I see" all the man was capable of offering?

Maybe he sees the work I did as inferior. Betsy couldn't believe how inconsequential she felt in this man's presence. She, who used to look down her nose at those she thought were beneath her, felt as out of place standing beside Rev. Covington as one of the canal mules trying to take up residence inside a church.

"Shall we be on our way?" he asked, pulling her thoughts back to the present.

She offered a quick nod then led the way to her buckboard.

This time Betsy allowed the reverend to help her climb aboard. She even offered to let him take the reins, but he declined, saying he could enjoy the scenery more if he wasn't driving.

Betsy took up the reins and got the horse moving again. They rode in silence for a time, until he turned to her and said, "The lay of the land is quite different here than in Buffalo. The navigation system is a whole different world, isn't it?" He pointed to a flat-roofed boat making its way up the canal with a load of coal.

"Yes it is, but there used to be a lot more action on the canal than there is now."

"Many things that were once hauled by the canal boats are now being transported by train," he said with a nod.

Her eyebrows lifted as she stared at him.

"When I was asked to interview here, I made an effort to learn about the area," he explained.

"I see." Betsy drew in a deep breath and decided to broach the subject she dreaded the most. "What kind of congregation are you looking for, Rev. Covington?"

"A needy one. A caring one." He paused and reached up to rub his chin. "A congregation that works together, plays together, and most importantly, prays together."

Betsy couldn't argue with that. She'd heard her father stress the importance of prayer to his flock many times.

"Now I have a question for you," he said.

"What's that?"

"How did you get involved with the Salvation Army, and what took you to New York City in the first place?"

Betsy spent the next little while telling William about her call to the mission field, how she'd been beaten and robbed when she first got to New York, and the details of Abigail nursing her back to health, then introducing her to the work and mission of the Salvation Army. "There are so many needy people in New York City, and if we can help even one find his way to Christ, it's worth every hour we spend serving others at the soup kitchens and conducting street meetings," she added.

"Any form of ministry that leads people to God is a worthy endeavor," he said with a note of conviction.

"I agree."

"I imagine your father missed you when you left for New York."

"I suppose he did. I was very involved at our church until

I went away." Betsy nodded toward the canal. "My father and I even held some services down here so the boatmen could hear God's Word. Papa would preach, and I played my zither and led the people in singing."

His eyebrows lifted high on his forehead. "Why don't the boatmen attend church in town?"

"Some do, but others aren't comfortable inside a church building."

"I see." He stared straight ahead. "That would make it hard for the church to grow. This could be a difficult ministry."

Betsy shrugged, wondering if he might have second thoughts about coming here to interview. "If the board of deacons asks you to take the church, how would your family feel about moving here?" she asked.

He turned and looked at her. "I have no family except my mother, father, and older brother who is married. If I take this church, none of my family will be coming with me, only Frances Bevens, an older widow who used to be my nanny and might be coming as my housekeeper."

"Oh, I see. I thought you might have a wife and children."

He grimaced, and the light in his eyes faded. "No, I'm as single as any man can be."

Chapter 4

❖

*A*s William headed down Main Street after leaving the small hotel where he'd spent the previous night, he thought about his meeting with Betsy Nelson the day before. She was obviously a devoted daughter, having left New York and given up a work she seemed passionate about in order to care for her father. William was sure it must have been difficult for her to meet him yesterday, since he could possibly be the one to take her father's place as shepherd of the community church.

His thoughts went to Betsy's father, the Rev. Hiram Nelson. The process of the church finding someone to replace him had to be even harder on the ailing man than it was on his daughter. Not only did Rev. Nelson have a serious health problem, but he'd been asked to give up his ministerial duties.

I haven't even begun my ministry as a pastor, William thought, *yet I would feel horrible if someone said I couldn't do it. Maybe I should stop by the reverend's house to speak with him and offer a word of encouragement.*

He reached into his jacket and withdrew the pocket watch that had once been his grandfather's. His meeting with the board of deacons was scheduled for ten o'clock at the church, and it was quarter to ten now. *I'd better wait to call on Rev. Nelson until after my interview,* he decided. *By then I'll know if I'll be taking his place.*

Betsy took one last look at her sleeping father and closed the door to his room. Dr. McGrath had been there earlier to examine Papa and give him some medicine to help him sleep.

Downstairs in the kitchen, Betsy stoked the woodstove and set a kettle of water on to heat. Maybe a cup of chamomile tea and some time in God's Word would help calm her nerves. She certainly needed something to take her mind off the interview that was going on in the church next door.

If Rev. Covington is asked to take Papa's position, I wonder how long it will be before he moves to Walnutport and we'll be expected to find a new home, she fretted.

Bristle Face, the shaggy terrier that had been her father's trusted friend for the last four years, flipped his tail against Betsy's long skirt and whined.

"What's the matter, boy?" she asked, reaching down to pet the animal's silky head. "Are you hungry, or do you need to go outside?"

The dog whimpered and padded across the room.

"All right then, out you go." Betsy hurried across the room, opened the door, and let out a squeal when she discovered Rev. Covington standing on the porch, dressed in a dark blue suit.

"Sorry if I startled you," he said. "I was getting ready to knock when you opened the door."

Before Betsy had a chance to respond, the little terrier stood on his hind legs and pawed at the man's pant leg.

"Bad dog! Get down," Betsy scolded as she gave Bristle Face a nudge with the toe of her shoe.

"It's okay. My father has an English setter, so I'm used to dogs." William chuckled. "Cats, too, for that matter."

Betsy bent down and scooped Bristle Face into her arms; then she stepped off the porch and placed him on the ground. "Now do your business, and be quick about it."

The dog turned, hopped back onto the porch, and pawed at William's pant leg again.

"Bristle Face, no!" she shouted. "I told you to stay down!"

William leaned over and picked up the terrier. "Bristle Face, huh? Interesting name."

Betsy gave a quick nod.

"I think the little guy has taken a liking to me."

"He can be a pest, but my father likes him." She smiled. "The dog showed up at the parsonage shortly after I moved to New York, and he's been Papa's friend ever since."

"Speaking of your father," William said, "I was wondering if I might have a few words with him."

"He's taking a nap right now."

"Would you mind if I wait until he wakes up? I'd like to speak with him about a few things."

"Is. . .is it about the church? Have the deacons decided to hire you?"

He nodded. "We've just finished the interview, and it was a unanimous decision."

Betsy felt the pounding of her heart against her rib cage, and she drew in a calming breath. "Have you accepted the call?"

"Yes. Yes I have."

Her heart continued to thud, and then it felt like it had sunk all the way to her toes. A new shepherd would soon lead Walnutport Community Church, and she and Papa would have to move.

William, still holding Bristle Face, took a step toward Betsy. "Are you all right? You look pale. Maybe you should sit down."

Betsy didn't want to sit. She didn't want to continue this discussion with the new minister. All she wanted to do was run into the house and have a good cry. But what good would that do? It wouldn't alter the fact that her father's life was about to change and hers right along with it. For Papa's sake she needed to remain strong.

Stepping onto the porch, Betsy nodded at the wooden bench positioned near the railing. "Won't you have a seat? I'll run inside and get some refreshments."

"Please, don't go to any bother."

"It's no bother. I'll be right back." She rushed into the house before Rev. Covington could say anything more.

When she returned a few minutes later with some tea and a plate of ginger cookies, she found Rev. Covington sitting on the bench with Bristle Face in his lap.

Betsy placed the tray on the small table near the bench and handed him a cup of tea.

He smiled and took a sip. "Umm. . .this is good."

She leaned against the porch railing and folded her arms. "Help yourself to some cookies."

"Aren't you having any?"

"I'm not really hungry."

He tapped the empty space beside him. "Then please have a seat. It makes me feel uncomfortable to watch you stand while I enjoy the fruits of your labor."

Betsy shrugged and seated herself on one end of the bench, being careful to put a respectable distance between them. "How soon will you be moving into the parsonage?"

"Probably not for another month. I'll need to return home to pack whatever things I'll need for the trip."

"When will you be heading to Buffalo?"

"On Monday morning. I'll be preaching tomorrow morning as planned. That way I'll have the chance to meet my new congregation before I head back."

Betsy flinched. Everything was happening so fast, and she dreaded having to give her father the news of the board's decision.

"When I asked one of the deacons about music in the church, he said his wife had been playing the organ while you were in New York, but now that you're back, she would prefer having you take over that responsibility again," William said.

"I. . .I suppose I could play on the Sundays Papa feels well enough to be in church or is up to staying home by himself." She sighed. "I'll make sure we're moved out of the parsonage by the time you get back from Buffalo."

Bristle Face woke up just then and jumped onto the porch. Rev. Covington shifted on the bench and turned to face Betsy. "If it were only me to worry about, I'd be happy to stay at one of the boardinghouses in town, but as I mentioned before, I'll be bringing my housekeeper along." His face turned a light shade of red. "It was Mother's idea. The moment I told her I was coming for an interview, she started planning things. She insists that, since I'm not married, I'll need to have someone to cook and keep house for me."

"Well, you needn't worry," Betsy was quick to say. "Papa and I will be moved out of the parsonage well before you and your housekeeper arrive."

A flutter of nervousness tickled William's stomach as he stepped onto the platform at the community church the following morning. In one month, this would be his church and the men and women staring back at him would be his people. It would be an exciting venture, yet a frightening one, since this was his very first church. He wanted to make a good impression.

He took a seat in one of the chairs near the back of the platform as Ben Hanson, the head deacon, stepped up to the pulpit. "Good morning," the man said in a booming voice, nodding at the congregation. "Yesterday the board of deacons met with Rev. Covington, and I'm happy to say that our vote was unanimous to call him as our new pastor." Ben motioned William to step forward. "I'm pleased to say that Rev. Covington has accepted that call."

William joined the deacon behind the pulpit, hoping his smile didn't appear forced and that his suit wasn't showing the signs of the perspiration he felt under his arms. "I'm glad to be here this morning," he said, nodding at the congregation.

His gaze went to the first row of pews, where Betsy Nelson sat, dressed in a pale yellow frock that matched the color of her hair. He noted that Betsy's father wasn't with her, and William figured the man either wasn't feeling well enough to attend church this morning or couldn't tolerate the idea of seeing someone else standing behind his pulpit.

Yesterday, when Rev. Nelson had awoken from his nap, William had been able to speak with him, and he'd been impressed by the man's friendliness. Yet he'd sensed a sadness that went deeper than Rev. Nelson's health problems, and William wondered what it could be.

"There wasn't time to plan a welcome dinner in honor of our new pastor today, but we'll have a short time of fellowship with coffee and cookies after the service so everyone has a chance to greet Rev. Covington," Ben said, giving William's shoulder a squeeze. "Tomorrow morning the good reverend will return to his home in Buffalo, but he'll back within the month to begin his ministry here in our little church."

The congregation clapped—everyone except Betsy Nelson, who sat stiff and tall with her hands folded in her lap. *She's probably not happy about me taking her father's place, and hearing the deacon's exuberant introduction must have been difficult for her.*

"Now, if you'll take your songbooks and turn to page 15, our song leader, Bill Hamilton, will lead us in praising the Lord." Ben stepped aside, and a young, dark-haired man wearing a well-worn suit stepped onto the platform. William returned to his seat behind the pulpit, Betsy took her place at the organ, and everyone rose to their feet.

When the first song, "The Solid Rock," began, William was surprised at the congregation's zeal for singing. Apparently this was a foot-stomping, hand-clapping group of people he'd agreed to pastor, and that would take some getting used to. The church William had grown up in back in Buffalo was full of people who barely smiled on Sunday mornings, and they certainly never would have shouted, "Hallelujah! Praise the Lord!"

He glanced over at Betsy, who was matching the rhythm of the music as her head bobbed up and down, and her feet pumped the pedals of the well-used organ that sat near the front of the room.

Yes indeed, William said to himself as he tapped his foot against the wooden platform, *this will surely take some getting used to.*

Chapter 5

———❖———

I think you and your father will be comfortable here," Freda
Hanson said as she opened the door to the small cottage
she'd offered to show Betsy. "Since my niece has recently
married and moved to Boston, the house is empty, and Ben
and I would be happy to have good people like you and your
father living here."

Betsy followed the tall, slender woman inside. Ben and
Freda, a middle-aged, childless couple, were among the few
people living in Walnutport who had been educated past
high school. Soon after he'd become a successful businessman
in Boston, Ben had decided to return to his hometown of
Walnutport and open a few businesses. The bank was one

of them, as well as a hotel, a restaurant, and a few small cottages.

"How much would the rent be?" Betsy asked as her gaze traveled around the small, partially furnished living room. "I don't have a job yet, and Papa won't be getting any more money from the church, so—"

Freda put her arm around Betsy's shoulder and gave it a gentle squeeze. "Now don't fret, dear. Ben and I have talked this over, and we want you and your father to live here rent free for as long as necessary. All we ask in return is that you keep the place clean and in good condition." She smiled. "It's the least we can do for the kindhearted man who pastored our church for so many years."

Betsy swallowed around the lump in her throat. "Your offer is so generous, but I was planning to get a job and—"

"Your father needs you to be close to him now," Freda interrupted. "Perhaps you can do sewing or laundry for some of the boatmen. That would be something you could do from home."

Betsy nodded as she fought to keep her emotions under control. "That might be best since I couldn't afford to hire someone to look out for Papa if I took a job away from home."

Freda gave Betsy's shoulder another squeeze. "Anytime you need to go shopping, run errands, or just take a break, be sure to let me know. I'll ask one of the ladies from church to stay with your father while you're gone."

"That's kind of you. I. . .I can't tell you how much I appreciate all you and Mr. Hanson have already done."

"Ben and I realize how hard this must be for you and your father. We want to do all we can to make this transition as smooth as possible." Freda motioned to the door leading to the next room. "Why don't I show you the rest of the house? Then if you think it's acceptable, we'll see about getting some of the men from church to move your things over right away. Our new preacher and his housekeeper will be in Walnutport by the end of the week, so we'll need to see that the parsonage is vacated before then."

Betsy didn't need any reminder that the new preacher was coming. It had been on her mind every day since Rev. Covington had left Walnutport after his call to their church. She blinked against stinging tears and bit her bottom lip, determined not to break down in front of Freda. *Papa and I will make it through this. With God's help, we can do it.*

———— ❋ ————

"This is the home the church has provided for the minister?" Mrs. Bevens's voice raised a notch as William followed her into the kitchen.

"It seems to be adequate for my needs." William and his housekeeper had arrived in Walnutport a short time ago, and he was showing her around the parsonage. "Having the home right next to the church makes it quite handy."

"You will no doubt want to entertain some of the town's more prominent business people in the hopes of getting them to support your church financially." She made a swooping gesture with one hand and cast a mournful look at the faded blue curtains hanging on the window above the sink. "This place isn't large enough or nice enough for entertaining a mere commoner, much less someone of higher standing."

"Most of the people living in Walnutport are not well-to-do, and this house is all the church has to offer, so we shall make the best of it." William leaned against the table and folded his arms. "If you're not happy with the arrangements, then perhaps you should catch the next train back to Buffalo and tell my mother you've changed your mind about being my housekeeper."

Mrs. Bevens patted the sides of her graying brown hair, pulled back into a perfectly shaped bun, and squinted her hazel eyes. "I'll simply have to make do. I'm sure that, once we're able to fill the house with some decent furniture and hang some proper curtains at the windows, the place will be a bit more livable."

William's gaze went to the ceiling. He could only imagine what kind of plans Mrs. Bevens had for this simple, warm home. Maybe if she kept busy with her remodeling projects, she wouldn't have time to smother him, the way she had done during his childhood.

A knock at the back door drove William's thoughts aside, and before Mrs. Bevens had a chance to respond, he strode across the room and opened the door. He discovered a middle-aged, dark-haired woman standing on the porch, holding a wicker basket.

"Afternoon, Pastor," she said with a friendly grin. "I'm Alice Clark, and my husband, Garth, and I are members of your church. We met on the Sunday after your interview, but you might not remember us, since that was a whole month ago."

William returned her smile. "I do remember, Mrs. Clark. If I'm not mistaken, you were the lady who made those wonderful oatmeal cookies."

Her head bobbed up and down as she held the basket out to him. "Those were mine, all right. I've brought you a tasty potato casserole today, along with a loaf of freshly baked bread."

"Thank you, Mrs. Clark. That was thoughtful of you." William opened the door wider. "Won't you come in and meet my housekeeper?"

"Only for a minute. I promised to do some shopping with my daughter Mabel this afternoon. Mabel teaches school here in Walnutport, and she's not married." Alice's pale blue eyes fairly twinkled. "We'll have you over for supper soon, so the two of you can get better acquainted."

William grimaced internally and stepped aside. If his role as minister was going to include lots of supper invitations, he might have to keep an eye on his weight. And if his ministerial duties included dodging matchmaking mothers and their available daughters, then at some point he might need to let his congregation know that he was a confirmed bachelor and planned to stay one.

As William stepped into the church on his first Sunday as pastor, deacons Ben Hanson and Henry Simms met him in the foyer. "Good morning, Rev. Covington," Ben said with a hearty handshake. "My wife wanted me to inform you that the ladies have planned a potluck dinner today, and it will be served on the lawn out behind the church after the service."

William smiled. "That's fine with me. My housekeeper isn't feeling well this morning, which is why she didn't accompany me to church, so I'm sure she won't feel up to cooking or attending the potluck."

Henry draped his arm across William's shoulder. "What you need is a wife, not a housekeeper, Rev. Covington."

A sour knot formed in William's stomach. *Don't tell me the men in this church want to match me up with their daughters, too. Maybe I should make the announcement about being a confirmed bachelor at the close of my sermon today.*

"Are you sure you're feeling up to going to the worship service this morning?" Betsy asked as she strolled down the

43

sidewalk with one hand in the crook of her father's arm. In the other hand she carried a basket full of muffins she had made for the potluck dinner. Papa seemed a little stronger this morning, but being back in church and seeing his successor standing behind the pulpit might be hard on him. She'd wanted him to stay home, but he'd adamantly refused, saying he was anxious to hear the new preacher deliver his sermon.

Papa gave Betsy's hand a reassuring squeeze. "I feel better today than I have in weeks."

"Maybe that's because you've been sleeping more lately."

"And maybe it's because my daughter is taking such good care of me."

She smiled. "I enjoy taking care of you. I'm just not looking forward to seeing someone else take your place."

"I'd like to see you get involved in some church activities," he said, making no reference to his replacement. "A bit of socializing would be good for you, Betsy."

"I didn't return to Walnutport so I could socialize. I'm here to see to your needs."

"Be that as it may, you still need to make time for some fun."

They were approaching the church, so Betsy decided to drop the subject.

A short time later they entered the sanctuary where several others had already gathered. Rev. Covington was seated in one of the chairs near the back of the platform.

Betsy escorted her father to a seat and hurried to take her place at the organ. When the song leader announced the first hymn, "Rescue the Perishing," Betsy's heart sank clear to her toes. This was a song she had often sung while she played her zither during street meetings in New York. It was a reminder of the call God had placed on her heart four years ago. Though she might not have gone to a foreign country as a missionary, she'd certainly met the challenge of spreading God's Word during her years with the Salvation Army, and she missed it.

What can I do to serve You here in Walnutport? Betsy beseeched the Lord as she opened her songbook to the proper page. *Is there anyone besides Papa to whom I can minister?*

Chapter 6

———※———

*Y*oo-hoo, Pastor Covington! Could you please come here a minute?"

William set his cup of coffee on the table and turned to see who had called him. Clara Andrews was waving frantically and looking wide-eyed and desperate. Maybe if he acted as if he hadn't heard, she would get busy talking to someone else and forget she had called him.

Ever since the potluck had begun, several women, and even a few men, had bombarded William with supper invitations and introduced their eligible daughters. It seemed to be a hazard of his chosen profession—at least the supper invitations. If he were married, dealing with desperate mothers and tethering young women wouldn't be a problem.

Maybe I should have made that announcement that I'm not a candidate for marriage. That would have saved these hopeful parents the trouble of introducing their daughters and planning some special meal in my honor. William grimaced. If he had made such an announcement, he might have some explaining to do. More than likely, people would have wanted to know why he was opposed to marriage, and he wasn't ready to share the shame of being left at the altar. Still, he wasn't willing to pretend he hadn't heard Mrs. Andrews call his name either.

As William stood, he glanced at Rev. Nelson, who sat beside his daughter at the next table. Hiram was probably the only parent present who hadn't tried to pawn his daughter off on the new preacher.

"Pastor Covington, are you coming?" Clara called again. This time she held a white hankie above her head and waved it as though it were a flag of surrender.

With a sigh of resignation, William ambled across the yard to see what the determined woman wanted.

When he arrived at the place where she and several other women stood, Clara pointed to a cluster of wooden boxes sitting beside one of the tables. "As a welcome gift, our church folks have put together some food items for you to take home so your pantry will be well stocked."

"Thank you," he said with a nod. "That was generous of

you." At least it wasn't another supper invitation in hopes of him getting together with someone's daughter.

"What's all this?" Mrs. Bevens asked as William entered the kitchen, carrying one of the boxes he'd been given during the potluck.

"Donations of food." He set the box on the sideboard near the sink. "Several more like it are on the porch."

Mrs. Bevens peeked into the box and wrinkled her nose. "Ten jars of blackstrap molasses! What am I supposed to do with those?"

"Use them for baking."

"Humph! I prefer to use honey when I bake."

William started for the door but turned when she spoke again.

"I see some home-canned vegetables in here, too. How do you know they were properly prepared and won't make us sick?"

He clenched his teeth. "I'm sure we won't die from food poisoning, Mrs. Bevens. But just to be sure, I'll say an extra prayer over each of our meals."

"I think to be on the safe side, I'll throw away the jars that don't look right to me."

"I wouldn't want to hurt anyone's feelings by throwing away what they've worked so hard to prepare."

Mrs. Bevens compressed her thin lips and squinted at the box, but before she could comment, William said, "By the way, what are you doing out of bed? You said you weren't feeling well this morning, and since you couldn't go to church, I figured you would spend the day resting."

Mrs. Bevens straightened to her full height, and her cheeks turned pink. "I *was* feeling under the weather, but I got up in order to fix your lunch."

"That was kind of you, but I have already eaten. We had a potluck meal after church." William patted his much-too-full stomach and grinned. "It didn't take me long to discover that there are some fine cooks in my congregation."

"Too many potlucks like that, and you'll end up looking like your father's friend Eustace Landers." Mrs. Bevens released an undignified grunt. "His stomach's so big that he has to sit a foot away from the table in order to eat. It's a wonder the poor man can even walk."

William went out the door, shaking his head. He returned to the kitchen moments later with another box of food, which he placed on the table.

Mrs. Bevens was immediately at his side, peering into the box as if it had been packed full of snakes. "You should see how many containers of salt are in here. Too much salt's not good for anyone."

"Too little salt makes everything taste flat," William mumbled under his breath.

She glared at him. "Are you insinuating that my cooking is flat?"

"Your cooking is fine, Mrs. Bevens." William rushed out of the room before she could say anything more.

"Are you sure you won't take a nap?" Betsy asked her father soon after they arrived home from church. "You look awfully tired."

He shook his head. "I'll just sit in my chair and read a few passages of scripture. If I get sleepy, I'll lie down on the sofa."

"All right. I'll go make some tea."

Betsy had just reached the door leading to the other room when he called out to her. "Do you know where Bristle Face is? I haven't seen him since we got home from church!"

"I tied him to a tree in the backyard before we left this morning. Since he's not used to our new home yet, I didn't want to take a chance that he might run off."

"Would you mind bringing my furry friend inside? I'd like to hold him awhile."

"Sure, Papa. I'll get him right now." Betsy scurried out of the room and went out the back door. When she reached the end of the porch, she halted. The rope she'd tied around Bristle Face's neck was still connected to the tree, but the dog wasn't on the other end of it.

She scanned the yard but didn't see Bristle Face anywhere. She cupped her hands around her mouth and hollered, "Bristle Face! Where are you, boy?"

No whine. No bark. No sign of the dog.

She ran around the side of the house, checking behind the shrubs, calling the dog's name, looking under the porch, and searching every nook and cranny. No Bristle Face. She was getting worried. What if the animal had run off and couldn't find his way back? She knew her father would be heartsick if he lost his loyal companion.

Betsy moaned and went back inside.

"Did you find him?" Papa asked as soon as she had entered the sitting room.

She shook her head. "Bristle Face broke free from his rope and took off. I searched the entire yard, but there was no sign of him."

Papa frowned. "It's not like my dog to take off. I wonder if. . ."

"What is it, Papa? What are you thinking?"

"Do you suppose Bristle Face went back to the parsonage? That's been his home ever since he was a pup. He might have gotten confused once he broke the rope, so he could have headed for the place he knows best."

"You might be right about that. Would you like me to go over there and see?"

He nodded. "If Bristle Face isn't there, would you ask the new preacher to keep an eye out for him—in case he shows up on his doorstep?"

"Of course." Betsy leaned over and kissed her father's forehead. "I'll be back soon."

As Betsy walked over to the parsonage, she searched for Bristle Face along the way. She saw no sign of the scruffy little black terrier, and none of the people she spoke with had seen the dog either.

Soon she reached the parsonage, and when she stepped onto the porch, the boards creaked under her feet. She lifted her hand and was about to knock when the door swung open. Rev. Covington stepped out, still wearing the dark gray suit he'd worn to church that morning. "I didn't realize anyone was here," he said.

"Actually I was about to knock when you opened the door."

She held his gaze for a moment, then, feeling a bit uncomfortable, looked away. The young minister's neatly trimmed hair and finely chiseled features seemed to fit his refined personality, and being in his presence made her feel like a commoner. "I hope I haven't interrupted anything," she mumbled, forcing herself to look at him again.

"No no. I was just on my way over to the church to get my Bible." His ears turned pink. "I got busy carrying the boxes of food and forgot it."

"I see."

"What can I do for you?" he asked. "Is it about your father? Is he doing all right this afternoon?"

She nodded. "He says he's fine, although I think the long day took a bit out of him."

"That's understandable."

Betsy shifted her weight and leaned against the porch railing. "The reason I came by is to ask if you've seen Papa's dog. I tied him to a tree in our backyard this morning, but he broke free while we were at church, and I thought he might have come here."

"He wasn't here when I got home, but I suppose he could be now. Shall we go around back and take a look?"

"Sure."

They stepped off the porch, and Rev. Covington's footsteps quickened through the tall grass as they made their way around the side of the house. They had just reached the backyard when Betsy's steps slowed, and she halted. "Look, there he is!" She pointed to the overgrown flower bed near the porch, where the dog lay curled in a tight ball.

The pastor patted the side of his knee. "Here, Bristle Face. Come here, little fella."

The dog lifted his head, stretched his front feet in front of him, and plodded across the yard. Rev. Covington bent down and scooped the animal into his arms. "You don't live here anymore," he said, ruffling the wiry hair on the terrier's head. "You've got to stay at your new home with your master now."

Betsy reached over and rubbed one of Bristle Face's silky ears. "I don't know if he showed up here because he still thinks it's his home or if it's because he's taken a liking to you, Rev. Covington."

"I'd appreciate it if you would call me Pastor William." He smiled, and the dimples in his cheeks seemed to deepen.

"All right, Pastor William," she murmured.

"It's nice to know someone likes me today," he said as he continued to pet the dog. "I think my housekeeper is ready to disown me."

Betsy tipped her head. "Why's that?"

He shrugged, and his ears turned even pinker. Betsy had a hunch it didn't take much to make the young minister blush.

"I shouldn't have asked," she said. "It's none of my business."

William handed her the dog. "Let's just say Mrs. Bevens and I had a difference of opinion."

Betsy didn't press the issue. She figured whatever had caused the rift between William and his housekeeper was between them. "I guess I'd better take this little guy home."

Pastor William placed his hand on Betsy's wrist. The innocent contact sent unexpected shivers up her arm.

"Did your father say anything about my sermon today?" he asked, apparently unaware of her reaction.

She blinked a couple of times. "Uh. . .no, he didn't. Why do you ask?"

"I wanted to be sure I didn't say anything he disapproved of."

Betsy drew in a couple of shallow breaths. "I. . .I'm sure Papa found no fault in your message."

A look of relief flashed onto his face, and he nodded. "That's good to hear."

She moistened her lips with the tip of her tongue. "I thought you did well with the delivery of your sermon, and the congregation can always use a reminder of the importance of unity."

"Thanks," he said with a smile that reached all the way to his dark blue eyes. "I appreciate hearing that."

Bristle Face stirred restlessly in Betsy's arms. "I. . .uh. . . really should go. Have a good afternoon, and I hope you locate your Bible as easily as I found Papa's dog."

He snickered, and they walked away in opposite directions. *I can see why so many women in church are anxious to match the new pastor with their daughters,* Betsy thought. *Despite the fact that I wish he weren't taking Papa's place, he is quite charming.*

Chapter 7

*T*he following morning, after Betsy had finished cleaning the kitchen and had washed a batch of clothes one of the boatmen had brought her, she decided to check on Bristle Face. She had tied him to a tree in the backyard again, being careful to make sure the knot was more secure than it had been the day before.

As Betsy stepped out the back door, the morning sun struck her shoulders with such intense heat that she grimaced. "I'll be glad when summer is over and fall brings in cooler weather." She squinted against the harsh light and scanned the yard until her gaze came to rest on the maple tree where she'd tied Bristle Face. The dog wasn't there. "Oh no," she moaned. "Not again."

Betsy trudged back to the house, mumbling all the way. She found her father in the sitting room, reclining on the sofa with his Bible in his hands. "Bristle Face has broken free from his rope again," she said. "I've a pretty good hunch where he's gone."

Papa turned his head toward her. "Maybe we should see if some of the men from church would be willing to put a fence around our yard. That's probably the only way we're going to keep that renegade dog from running back to the parsonage all the time."

"I'll speak to the new pastor about it when I go over to get Bristle Face. Hopefully he'll be willing to round up a crew of men to do the work." Betsy nodded at her father. "I'm sure you would do the same thing for someone if you were still the pastor."

"I'd do more than that. I would be the first one in line to do the work."

A pang of regret stabbed Betsy's heart as she was reminded once more of the reality of her father's declining health. The doctor had told her that any day Papa could have another heart attack and the next one could be his last. "Will you be all right on your own? I really should go over to the parsonage and retrieve Bristle Face before he makes a nuisance of himself."

He smiled. "I'll be fine, so there's no need to hurry back if you decide to stay and visit awhile."

"I shouldn't be too long." Betsy leaned over and kissed the top of his head before she left the room.

A short time later she found herself on the front porch of the parsonage, knocking on the door.

When the door opened, she was greeted by a tall, older woman with hazel eyes and graying brown hair worn in a tight bun at the back of her head. "May I help you?"

"Is Pastor William in? I need to speak with him."

"He's not here right now." The woman nodded curtly. "I'm his housekeeper, Mrs. Bevens. Is there something I can help you with?"

The intensity in the woman's eyes made Betsy feel like a bug about to be squashed. She shifted her weight from one foot to the other. "I'm Betsy Nelson, and I'm here about my father's dog, Bristle Face. He broke free from his rope again, and I thought he might have come here."

Mrs. Bevens squinted as she stared at Betsy. "Are you sure you're not using the dog as an excuse to see William?"

"What? I assure you that—"

"Two other young women have already called on the pastor this morning," Mrs. Bevens said, cutting Betsy off in midsentence. She lifted her chin and held her shoulders rigid. "Of course, they made up some excuse about needing to know if the pastor planned to begin a choir, and if so, they wanted him to know they were willing to be in it."

"I only came to see if my father's dog is here," Betsy said with a shake of her head. "He came over to the parsonage yesterday afternoon, and since he's broken free again, I thought he might have—"

"I don't know anything about a dog." Mrs. Bevens pursed her lips. "Rev. Covington is at the church going over some music, so I'm sure he won't want to be disturbed. Good day to you, Miss Nelson." With that, the woman pivoted on her heel and shut the door.

Betsy stood with her mouth hanging open. She'd never met such a rude, irritating woman. Even during her most self-centered days, she hadn't acted that unpleasantly. At least she hoped she hadn't.

She turned and started down the porch steps. *Maybe I'll head over to the church and speak to Pastor William. At least I can let him know that Bristle Face has escaped again and might turn up on his doorstep.*

For the last half hour, William had been sitting on a back pew in the sanctuary, looking through the hymnbook, and he still hadn't found the song he was searching for. His message next week would be on the subject of hope, and he'd planned to sing a solo before he spoke to the congregation.

When William heard a door open and close, he set the hymnal aside and walked to the foyer. Betsy Nelson stood there, her flaxen hair hanging down her back in soft, gentle waves, rather than being pulled back in its usual bun, and he drew in a quick breath, surprised by her beauty. "Good—good morning, Betsy." His voice sounded strained, and he cleared his throat a couple of times, giving himself a good mental shake. "How may I help you?"

Her cheeks blushed crimson, and she averted her gaze. "Bristle Face is missing again. I stopped by the parsonage to see if he'd gone there, but your housekeeper said she hadn't seen him."

William tapped his chin with the tip of his finger. "Mrs. Bevens doesn't much care for dogs. If Bristle Face did show up there, she probably chased him away."

Betsy's stunned expression made him wish he could take back his words, so he quickly added, "I'm sure she would have told you if she'd seen him though."

"I hope he hasn't run away or become lost," she said. "It would break Papa's heart if something happened to his little terrier."

Betsy looked so forlorn that, for one crazy moment, William had the impulse to give her a hug. *Take control of your thoughts,* he reprimanded himself. *She might misinterpret the gesture, and besides, it wouldn't be appropriate.* "Is there any place the dog might have gone?" he asked. "Somewhere he's run off to before?"

"The only place he ever went when we lived next door was over here to the church," she said with a shrug.

William's eyebrows lifted in surprise. "Really? The dog came to church?"

"He didn't actually come to church; he just liked to follow my father over here when he came to prepare his sermons. Papa sometimes let Bristle Face into his study." Betsy chuckled. "Of course, no one but the two of us knew about that."

William grinned and touched his lips. "You can count on me to keep it a secret."

"So I take it you haven't seen any sign of the dog today?"

He shook his head. "I've been here for the last half hour, trying to find a song to share with the congregation before my message next Sunday."

"Are you looking for anything in particular?"

"I'll be speaking on the subject of hope."

"How about 'I Know Whom I Have Believed'? I'm quite sure it's on page 35 in our songbooks."

"That's impressive. You must be quite familiar with the hymnal."

"I've sung it several times at various Salvation Army street meetings."

He motioned toward the sanctuary. "Would you be willing to sing it for me now?"

Betsy nodded, although her face had turned quite pink.

He opened the door to the sanctuary and allowed her to go in first, then he followed her up front.

Betsy took a seat on the organ bench, and William sat on the front pew. He watched as she set the hymnal on the music rack and turned to the proper page. Her legs began pumping, her fingers pressed down on the keys, and the room swelled with mellow music. He closed his eyes and rested against the pew as her voice sang out:

> *"I know not why God's wondrous grace*
> *To me He hath made known,*
> *Nor why, unworthy, Christ in love*
> *Redeemed me for His own.*
>
> *"But I know whom I have believed,*
> *And am persuaded that He is able*
> *To keep that which I've committed*
> *Unto Him against that day."*

When she began the second verse, he joined in:

> *"I know not how this saving faith*
> *To me He did impart,*
> *Nor how believing in His Word*
> *Wrought peace within my heart."*

He stood and moved over to the organ.

> *"But I know whom I have believed,*
> *And am persuaded that He is able*
> *To keep that which I've committed*
> *Unto Him against that day."*

They finished the next three verses as a duet, and when the song was over, William sank to the bench beside her. "You have the voice of an angel, do you know that? It should be you singing the solo next Sunday, not me."

"Maybe we could sing the song together," she said in a voice barely above a whisper.

"I would like that."

Chapter 8

——◆❖◆——

*O*n Sunday morning, as Betsy secured the rope that would tie Bristle Face to the maple tree in their backyard, she thought back to Monday and what had happened after she and William had finished practicing their song. Betsy had said she needed to get home to check on her father, and as she left the church, she'd found Papa's dog crouched in the bushes near the front porch of their cottage. She was relieved to see that Bristle Face wasn't hurt, but from the way he whined and crawled to her on his belly, she could tell something had traumatized him. It had made her wonder if the poor animal had gone over to the parsonage and been chased off by Pastor William's disagreeable housekeeper.

"You'd better stay put today," Betsy warned Bristle Face. "If you don't, I'll ask someone to build you a cage." She shook her head as she walked away, realizing she'd been so busy with laundry and mending jobs all week she'd forgotten to ask the pastor about finding someone to put a fence around their backyard. *I'll do that sometime this week,* she promised herself.

Returning to the house, Betsy found her father sitting on the sofa with his Bible lying open in his lap. It seemed as if he was always reading God's Word. "Are you sure you don't want to take the buckboard to church today?" she asked. "There's still time for me to hitch up the horse."

He shook his head. "I'd rather walk. The fresh air and sunshine are good for me; the doctor said so."

"All right then, but we still have plenty of time before church starts, so let's not be in a hurry getting there." Betsy touched his pale cheek. "Those dark circles under your eyes lead me to believe you didn't sleep well last night."

"I'll be fine." Papa closed his Bible and stood. "Shall we go?"

She nodded and slipped her hand into the crook of his arm.

As Betsy and her father headed to church, she became more concerned, because he had to stop every few feet in order to catch his breath.

"Maybe we should go back and get the buckboard," she suggested. "Or better yet, why don't you stay home from church today and rest?"

He shook his head. "And miss hearing you sing?"

Betsy smiled despite her growing concerns. Ever since Mama had died, Papa had doted on her. *Guess maybe he spoiled me a bit, too,* she mused, gripping her father's arm a little tighter as they proceeded down the street.

They were nearly at the church when Betsy halted. A trickle of perspiration rolled down her forehead and onto her nose. "Papa, do you think anyone in the congregation will get the wrong idea when Pastor William and I sing our duet?"

He stared at her like she'd taken leave of her senses. "Of course not, Betsy. Think of all the times you've sung with other people in our church, including me."

"But I wasn't sharing a song with a handsome, single minister."

Papa raised his bushy eyebrows. "Are you saying I'm not handsome?"

"Certainly not. You're the most handsome man I know." She smiled up at him. "But seriously, some people might wonder why the minister chose to sing with me. There might be those who will think there's something going on between Pastor William and me."

Papa grinned. "Is there something going on?"

"Absolutely not. We barely know each other, and I have no intention of—"

"You deserve to be happy, daughter. And when I'm gone,

you'll need to begin a life of your own."

She patted his arm. "I have a life, right here with you."

"I appreciate your devotion, but it's past time for you to find a husband and start a family of your own."

Betsy shook her head. "If the Lord was going to give me a husband, I'm sure He would have done so by now. I'm thirty-one years old, Papa, and no man has ever shown the slightest interest in me."

"What about Mike Cooper? He seemed interested for a time."

"Puh! It was me who was interested in Mike, not the other way around. He only had eyes for Kelly, and I was a fool to throw myself at him the way I did." Betsy lifted her chin as they walked up the steps leading to the church. "I'm older and wiser now, and I shall never do such a humiliating thing again."

William was glad Mrs. Bevens had come to church today, but he wasn't pleased with the dour expression on her face as she stood off to one side of the foyer, watching him greet people as they entered the building. *She's probably scrutinizing everything I say and do. I think if she didn't have something in which to find fault, she would be miserable.*

Turning away from Mrs. Bevens and her accusing stare, William stepped forward and greeted Betsy and her father.

"Good morning. How are you feeling today, Rev. Nelson?"

"I'm a bit winded from the walk over here, but I'm sure I'll be fine once I'm seated."

William glanced at Betsy to gauge her reaction.

"I tried to talk him into staying home today, but he insisted on coming." She frowned. "I couldn't get him to agree to take the buckboard, either."

"My daughter worries too much," Hiram said before William could offer a reply. He squeezed Betsy's shoulder. "I'm anxious to hear the song you and Betsy will be singing today. She has a beautiful voice, and from what I hear, so do you."

William smiled, and he glanced at Mrs. Bevens again. She gave him an angry glare, as if to remind him of what she had told him that morning during breakfast. "I'm concerned about how your duet with Miss Nelson will look to the congregation," she had said. When he asked what she meant, she had pursed her lips, then replied, "Some people might get the impression that you're romantically interested in Betsy, and if you choose to sing with her, it might set off some ugly rumors."

He had assured Mrs. Bevens that he had no romantic interest in any woman and that he'd only asked Betsy to help with the song because she sang it so well and would keep him on key. He'd also said that he didn't believe the people in Walnutport were like those who lived in the larger cities, where vicious gossipers seemed to be everywhere. He'd ended the conversation by saying that if he got wind of any gossip in his church, he would be quick to nip it in the bud.

When William glanced at Mrs. Bevens again, he was relieved to see that she was now engaged in a conversation with Sarah Turner, one of the lock tenders' wives.

"We should get into the sanctuary," Betsy said, taking hold of her father's arm. "Pastor William has other people to greet, and I need to get the organ warmed up."

As Betsy and her father moved away, the room seemed stuffy all of a sudden, and William slid one finger under the back of his shirt collar, noticing that it felt kind of tight. *Oh Lord,* he prayed, *please tell me I didn't do the wrong thing by asking Betsy to sing with me this morning.*

Betsy hadn't been sure if she could get through the music part of the service without making obvious mistakes, but she'd managed to play all the hymns as well as the offertory without missing a note. The pastor had offered a lengthy prayer after the congregational singing, and he'd just announced that he and Betsy would now sing a duet.

Dear Lord, she prayed, *please still my racing heart and help my voice not to crack in the middle of our song.*

As William stepped up to the organ, Betsy glanced at the congregation and noticed her father slouched on the front pew. He seemed to be struggling to keep awake, and she wished once more that he had stayed home in bed. Her gaze went to the other side of the room, where Mrs. Bevens sat rigid without a hint of a smile on her face.

Betsy grimaced internally. *For some reason that woman doesn't like me. Either that or she had a bowl of sour cherries for breakfast this morning.*

"I'm ready when you are," William whispered, bending close to Betsy's ear.

She nodded, and a shiver tickled her spine.

Betsy sang the first verse alone, and William joined her on the chorus. Their voices blended in perfect unison, and Betsy soon forgot her nervousness as she allowed the music and the words of the beautiful hymn to lift her spirits. As they reached the last note, she felt as if God was looking down from heaven and smiling His approval.

The room exploded with applause and numerous *amen*s, and everyone but William's housekeeper and a few of the young, single women smiled back at them.

When the service ended and Betsy and her father headed for the door, she was stopped by several people who said how much they enjoyed the duet. Some even commented on how well the pastor's and Betsy's voices blended, and Kelly Cooper had been bold enough to whisper that she thought Betsy and the preacher looked real handsome together.

"Please don't tell that to the pastor or anyone else," Betsy whispered back. "I wouldn't want any false rumors getting started."

"Oh, don't worry," Kelly said as she ushered her two children out the door behind their father. "I would never embarrass you that way."

Betsy turned to her father, who looked even paler than he had earlier. "Should I see if someone can give us a ride home?"

He nodded. "That's probably a good idea. I'm feeling a bit weak and shaky."

"Why don't I walk you back to the sanctuary so you can have a seat? Then I'll see who might be available to take us home."

Papa took hold of Betsy's arm and offered her a feeble-looking smile. "You're such a thoughtful daughter, and you've got the voice of an angel. I know everyone enjoyed the song you and the pastor sang today."

"Thank you, Papa." Betsy saw that her father was situated on a back pew, and then she headed back to the foyer. She was about to ask Sarah Turner and her husband, Sam, if they could catch a ride in their wagon, when she overheard Clara Andrews invite the preacher over to her house for Sunday dinner. "It will give you and my daughter, Hortence, a chance to get better acquainted," the woman said, clasping the pastor's arm.

"I—I don't know." Pastor William looked kind of flustered. Had he made other plans for the afternoon? "I'll have to check with my housekeeper and see what plans she's made for our dinner today."

"Mrs. Bevens is welcome to join us. In fact, that will work out real well. She and I can visit while you and Hortence spend some time together."

And I was worried that someone might think I'd set my cap for the pastor, Betsy thought with a shake of her head. *I would say Pastor William is the one who needs to worry.*

Chapter 9

I'm heading out to make a few calls on some people in my congregation," William told Mrs. Bevens as he grabbed his Bible and started for the back door.

She looked up from the letters she'd been writing at the kitchen table and frowned. "Can't that wait? I was hoping you would help me measure the windows in the sitting room today. The curtains are terribly faded, and they should have been replaced before we moved in. I want to have some new ones put up as soon as possible."

"I don't think new curtains are a priority right now," he said with a wave of his hand.

"Oh, but they are," Mrs. Bevens argued. "If you're going

to entertain properly, you'll need the parsonage to look as nice as possible." She wrinkled her nose, as though some foul odor had permeated the room. "This house is a disgrace."

William grimaced. It was a shame that the persnickety woman put so much emphasis on material things and didn't seem to care about people or their needs. *And she calls herself a Christian,* he thought with dismay. *But then, it's not my place to judge. Only God has the right to do that.*

"I need to go, Mrs. Bevens. We'll talk about the curtains some other time." Without waiting for her reply, he rushed out the door.

Betsy pushed a strand of hair away from her face and bent to pick up a pair of trousers. She'd spent four hours last night at the treadle sewing machine, mending several shirts, which had left the muscles in her shoulders sore and tense. This morning after breakfast she'd come out to the backyard, where she'd spent several more hours stooped over the washtub, scrubbing trousers, shirts, and socks that had been dropped off by some of the boatmen on their way up the canal to Mauch Chunk. It was amazing how quickly the news had gotten out that Betsy was taking in clothes to wash and mend. While she wasn't earning a lot of money, it was enough for their basic needs, and since Papa had saved a little from his years of preaching, they could fall back on that if the need arose. Betsy felt sure that God would provide for their needs, and as much as she missed her work with the Salvation Army, at least she was doing something meaningful.

In order to make the time pass more quickly and to take her mind off the pain that had settled in her lower back, Betsy decided to sing a few hymns. She'd just finished "Almost Persuaded" and had just begun to sing "Only Trust Him," when a deep voice coming from the other side of the yard sang out, " 'Come, every soul by sin oppressed; there's mercy with the Lord, and He will surely give you rest by trusting in His Word.' "

Betsy turned and saw Pastor William walking across the grass, holding his Bible in one hand. "It's a beautiful song. Let's sing the refrain together," he said, as he approached her.

Betsy strummed the washboard, keeping time to the music as her voice blended with Pastor William's. " 'Only trust Him, only trust Him, only trust Him now; He will save you, He will save you, He will save you now.' "

When the song was over, she straightened and faced him, feeling the heat of a blush sweep over her face. "What brings you by on this hot, sticky morning?" she asked the smiling preacher.

He lifted his Bible. "I've been out calling on people. I hope to get into a routine of doing that at least once a week. I'll be setting certain hours aside for studying my sermon, too, of course."

Betsy resumed her scrubbing. "Have you given any thought to holding services along the canal for the boatmen and their families who don't come to the church?"

"I have considered the idea, but I'm wondering if it wouldn't be better if I went down to the canal, introduced myself, and invited those people to attend our regular Sunday services here in town. I understand that none of the canal boats run on Sunday, so I don't see why the boatmen can't come to the church."

Betsy grabbed another pair of trousers and sloshed them up and down in the soapy water. "I know many of the men who work the canals, and most wouldn't feel comfortable sitting inside a church building."

The pastor's eyes narrowed. "Why is that?"

"Most of the canalers don't have a lot of money. They wear simple, plain clothes, speak crudely, are uneducated, and would feel as out of place sitting on a polished pew as a duck trying to make its nest in a tree." She reached around to rub the kink in her back and winced.

"Are you in pain?" he asked, kneeling beside her with a look of concern.

"I'll be all right. It's just a little crick."

He glanced at the pile of wet clothes in the wicker basket beside the laundry tub. "Surely these can't all be your father's."

She shook her head. "I'm taking in washing and mending for some of the boatmen who don't have wives traveling with them. It was the only way I could think of to earn money."

He cringed, as though it were his back that hurt and not hers. "In the home where I grew up, we had servants to do our washing, mending, and other chores around the house. The most menial tasks I ever saw my mother do was to tend her rose garden and crochet lace doilies." He shook his head. "You shouldn't have to work so hard, Betsy. Not when you have your father to care for."

"I'm managing," she mumbled.

"Maybe my housekeeper could come by once a week to help you."

Betsy straightened to her full height, ignoring the pain that shot through her back. "Absolutely not! I can't afford to pay anyone, and I'm getting by fine on my own." She knew her tone was harsh, and she bit her bottom lip, wishing she could retract the words. "I—I'm sorry for snapping."

"It is I who should apologize. I'm sorry if I've offended you by my suggestion." Pastor William took a step closer to Betsy, and the scent of his spicy cologne stirred something deep within her.

"I tend to be a little too sensitive," she admitted, leaning away. "I think it comes from years of self-reproach."

He squinted his blue eyes. "Would you care to explain?"

Betsy stared at the ground. How could she admit that she used to be a flirt and had actually tried to manipulate men in order to get her way? She would be too embarrassed to confess that she'd once thrown herself at Mike Cooper, only to be rebuffed by him.

"I'm thinking the real reason you're a bit sensitive has more to do with your concern for your father than anything else. You seem like a loving, caring daughter, and your willingness to do such hard work is proof of that." He motioned to the washtub.

She shrugged. "Maybe, but I must confess that I wasn't always so loving or caring. In my younger days I was a selfish, spoiled girl, and my tongue was sharper than any fisherman's knife."

"People change, and you obviously have, for I don't see a trace of selfishness in you now."

Betsy rinsed the trousers in the bucket of water sitting beside the washtub, wrung them out, and placed them in the wicker basket. "Papa's in the house, resting on the sofa. I assume you came by to see him."

He nodded and raked his fingers through the back of his hair. "I also came to ask you a favor."

"Oh?"

He shifted from one foot to the other. "I was talking with Kelly Cooper when I stopped by the store this morning, and she mentioned that you used to do volunteer work at an orphanage in New York City."

"That's right. Several women from the Salvation Army helped out there."

He cleared his throat and rubbed his hand across his chin. "I figure if you've worked with orphans that you must have a special way with children."

"I never used to like children much. They made me feel uncomfortable," Betsy admitted. "But my work at the orphanage changed that, and now I realize how special children are."

"Yes, they're all precious in God's sight." Pastor William cleared his throat. "The thing is I paid a call on Andy and Mae Gates this morning. Mae is in a family way and hasn't been feeling well, so she's going to give up teaching her Sunday school class." He kicked a small stone with the toe of his shoe. "I was wondering if you might be willing to take over that class."

Betsy thought about the puppets she'd made to entertain the children at the orphanage and wondered if something like that might work for a Sunday school class of young girls. "I would be willing to teach," she finally said, "but my only concern is that I might not be able to be in church every week."

"You mean because of your father's health?"

She nodded.

"On the Sundays you feel you must stay at home, perhaps one of the other ladies from church could fill in as your substitute teacher." He smiled. "Or maybe someone could sit with your father while you're at church."

"I'd feel better staying with him when he's having a bad day," she said, nearly choking on the words. Betsy hadn't admitted it to anyone, but she was worried that Papa might not have much longer to live. She wanted to spend as much time with him as possible and was concerned that he might become extremely ill or could even die while she was away.

"I understand." Pastor William glanced at the house. "I'd best see how your father is doing now. Think about the Sunday school class and let me know, all right?"

"Yes, I will. Thank you for stopping by."

"You're welcome." He started for the house, whistling a hymn, and Betsy resumed her work, praying that the Lord would help her make a wise decision. She also prayed that God would allow her to spend many more days with her father.

Chapter 10

I'm glad you were able to come over for supper tonight," Clara Andrews said as William entered her modest but pleasant home. "But I'm sorry that your housekeeper isn't with you."

William nodded, wishing he didn't have to offer an explanation. "Mrs. Bevens sends her greetings, but she's been fighting a headache all day and didn't think she would be good company this evening." While it was true that Mrs. Bevens had told William she had a headache, he was pretty sure the real reason she hadn't come with him tonight was because she didn't want to socialize with anyone from his congregation. She thought she was better than them and had tried to convince William that most of the people he'd come to pastor in Walnutport were uneducated and lacked all the social graces she felt were so important.

"My daughter, Hortence, is in the sitting room," Clara said, gesturing to the room on her right. "Please, make yourself comfortable, and the two of you can visit while I get supper on the table."

William scanned the hallway, then he glanced into the sitting room. Seeing no sign of Clara's husband, Frank, he asked, "Where's Mr. Andrews?"

"Frank's out in the barn, feeding the animals. He should be done soon, I expect."

"Maybe I should go out and keep him company or see if I can help in any way."

"No no, that's not necessary. My husband prefers to do his chores alone." Clara grabbed hold of William's arm and practically shoved him toward the sitting room.

William felt like a bug trapped in a spider's web as he entered the room and took a seat in the chair closest to the door. Hortence, who sat on the sofa across from him, looked up from the needlepoint lying in her lap and smiled.

William nodded and forced a smile in return.

"You two have a nice visit." Clara ducked quickly out of the room before William had a chance to respond.

He shifted uncomfortably on the straight-backed chair as Hortence stared at him, the ends of her thin lips turning up, and her lashes blinking rapidly against her faded blue eyes. While the young woman wasn't what William would refer to as homely, she was certainly no beauty, either. Hortence's pale skin made him wonder if she ever spent any time outdoors, and her mousy brown hair, parted straight down the middle and pulled back into a tight bun, looked dry and brittle.

Say something, he admonished himself. *Anything to break the silence.* He cleared his throat a couple of times. "What's that you're working on, Hortence?"

Her smile widened as she lifted the piece of material and held it at arm's length. "It's going to be a pillow top—for my hope chest."

"I see." He loosened the knot on his tie a bit and squinted at the colorful needlepoint. "Is that a cluster of red roses?"

She nodded. "I hope to carry a bouquet of roses like this when I get married. Of course, I have to find a husband first," she added with an unladylike snicker.

William cringed. He hoped she wasn't hinting that he might be a candidate as her future husband. "I'm. . .uh. . . sure when the right man comes along, you'll make a lovely bride," he mumbled.

Hortence's eyes brightened, and she sat a little straighter, lifting her chin. "You really think so, Pastor William?"

"Of course. I've never seen a bride who wasn't lovely." An uninvited vision of Beatrice popped into his mind. William had never seen his fiancée in her wedding gown, but he was sure she would have been a beautiful bride. Even though it had happened several months ago, the thought of her leaving him at the altar still hurt like a festering sliver. Hardly a day went by that he didn't relive that discomforting moment, and he wondered once more if he would ever get over the humiliation of being rejected by the woman to whom he had pledged his undying love.

William clenched and unclenched his fingers around the arm of the chair. If he needed to remind himself a hundred times a day, he would never allow that to happen again.

"Mother says that because of my planning and organizational skills I would make a good preacher's wife," Hortence said, pulling his thoughts aside.

Unsure of how best to reply to the woman's bold comment, William stood and moved quickly to the unlit fireplace. He peered at the clock on the mantel. "I wonder what's keeping your father," he said when the clock bonged six times. "I thought he would have joined us by now."

Hortence sighed, and William turned to face her again. "Daddy always goes out to feed the animals just before supper, and he usually takes his time doing it. I would never say this to Mother, but I think he dawdles on purpose, just to get under her skin."

William glanced toward the adjoining room, which he assumed was the kitchen. He wondered if the Andrews couple might be having some kind of marital discord and, if so, whether they would feel comfortable talking to him about it.

He shifted his weight and glanced at the clock again. When he'd accepted the call to Walnutport, he hadn't given much thought to all the details that went with a minister's job. During his time at seminary, he'd concentrated on Bible studies, theology, church history, and learning how to deliver a sermon properly. He knew that counseling and being available to the people in his flock during illness and bereavement were an important part of his ministry, but until he'd taken a church, he hadn't realized how unprepared he was for it all.

He glanced over at Hortence again, who kept staring at him in such a peculiar way, and wondered if he might have a spot of dirt on his suit coat. He opened his mouth, prepared to ask, when she blurted out, "I'm wondering why such a handsome man as yourself isn't married yet, Pastor."

Heat flooded William's face, and he drew in a quick breath, hoping to diffuse the blush he knew must be covering his cheeks. "I'm. . .uh. . .that is. . . ."

"Don't you think it would make your ministry stronger if you had a helpmate?"

A trickle of sweat rolled down his face and dribbled under his shirt collar. "The biblical account of the apostle Paul leaves us with the impression that he wasn't married, yet he had a very successful ministry," he said in defense.

"That may be true, but—"

"Don't you usually help your mother with supper, Hortence?"

Hortence's mouth dropped open like a broken hinge. "Of course, but Mother said I should entertain you and that she would manage without my help this evening."

"I see." William sank into the chair, resigned to the fact that this was going to be a long evening. He hoped not all his supper invitations would turn out like this, and he prayed that God would help him remember to be friendly and sociable with everyone in the congregation, even the outspoken members like Hortence Andrews.

Betsy picked up the small, oval-shaped looking glass from her dressing table and peered at her reflection. Not wishing to appear too stiff and formal, she'd decided to wear her hair down today, secured at the back of her neck with a green ribbon that matched the high-necked, full-skirted cotton dress she had chosen.

"I hope I was right to agree to teach a Sunday school class," she murmured as she set the mirror down and moved across the room to fetch her shawl and the satchel full of teaching supplies.

For most of the week, Betsy had wrestled with the idea of whether it would be good for her to teach the girls' class.

Not until Papa said he thought she should do it and had assured her that he would be fine at home on the days he felt too tired to go to church had Betsy finally decided to give it a try. She knew she could either call on a substitute to teach the class or ask one of the ladies from church to come to their house and sit with Papa should it become necessary.

On Friday afternoon Betsy had gone to the parsonage and given the pastor her answer. He'd seemed pleased and said that if Betsy felt ready, she could begin teaching this Sunday.

"I'm ready," she murmured, gathering her hand puppets and slipping them into the satchel. She moved back to the dresser and, with one last look in the mirror, hurried out of the room.

She hoped Papa might feel up to going to Sunday school with her this morning, but when she stepped into the living room and found him asleep in his favorite chair, she felt a keen sense of disappointment. How different things were now than when she was a young girl. Back then, Papa had risen early every Sunday morning and had never missed teaching the men's Sunday school class or preaching to the congregation he cared so much about.

I'd best let him sleep, she decided. *Maybe he will feel up to coming to church if he rests awhile.*

Betsy tiptoed out of the room and opened the front door, feeling a mixture of excitement and apprehension about teaching a group of girls she barely knew. Would the children be eager to learn the Bible story she planned to tell them? Would they welcome her as their new teacher?

"I guess there's only one way to find out," Betsy said with a lift of her chin; then she stepped out the door.

Chapter 11

*I*f you won't let me take you to see the doctor, then I'm going to ask him to come over here and examine you," Betsy told her father Monday morning as they sat at the breakfast table.

"I'll be fine. I'm just a little more tired than usual, that's all."

"A little more tired?" Betsy pointed to the bowl of oatmeal sitting before him, untouched. "You stayed home from church yesterday because you felt tired; you ate very little supper last night; and you've been sitting at the table for half an hour without touching your tea, oatmeal, or your favorite cinnamon muffins."

"I'm not hungry." Papa's face looked paler than normal, and dark circles had formed beneath his eyes. He leaned forward, placing his elbows on the table and resting his forehead against the palms of his hands.

"Are you in pain?"

"Just some pressure in my chest, and I'm having a hard time getting my breath."

Betsy jumped up from the table. "That doesn't sound good to me, Papa. You need to see the doctor today!"

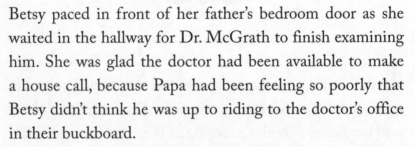

Betsy paced in front of her father's bedroom door as she waited in the hallway for Dr. McGrath to finish examining him. She was glad the doctor had been available to make a house call, because Papa had been feeling so poorly that Betsy didn't think he was up to riding to the doctor's office in their buckboard.

Oh Lord, she silently prayed, *please help Dr. McGrath think of something that might help Papa's heart grow stronger. I've only been home a few weeks, and I can't stand the thought of losing him.* She stopped in front of his bedroom door, tempted to poke her head inside and see what was taking so long.

Loud barking from outside drew Betsy's attention, and she moved over to the window at the end of the hall to look into the backyard. She spotted Bristle Face running back and forth, pulling on his rope, and yapping at two young boys who were walking by the house.

"I still need to see if someone will build us a fence. If something's not done, that dog will keep breaking free and running back to the parsonage." She shook her head. "That sure wouldn't set well with William's housekeeper."

The door to Papa's bedroom opened just then, and Betsy whirled around. "Dr. McGrath, how's my father doing?"

The doctor joined her at the window. "I'm afraid his heart has become weaker."

"Is. . .is he going to die?" Betsy hated to ask the question, but it had been on her mind ever since she'd returned to Walnutport.

"Short of a miracle, I'm afraid his heart won't hold out much longer." The doctor pursed his lips. "What Hiram needs is a new heart, but since that's not possible, the best we can do is make him comfortable and see that he gets plenty of rest."

Betsy drew in a shuddering breath. She thought she had prepared herself for this, but hearing the truth hurt worse than she could have imagined. "It doesn't seem right to give up hope," she said in a quavering voice.

"Perhaps we should go into the sitting room," Dr. McGrath said. "I'd like to discuss something with you."

Betsy nodded and led the way down the hall. When they entered the sitting room, the doctor placed his leather bag on the table by Papa's chair and took a seat. Betsy seated herself on the sofa across from him. "What is it you wish to talk to me about?" she asked.

"I recently read an article that was published in the *New York Medical Journal*," Dr. McGrath replied. "It's about an extract made from hawthorn berries, and it's used to treat various heart conditions."

Betsy leaned forward as a feeling of hope welled in her soul. "Has there been some success with this extract?"

"Some. Of course, it's still in the experimental stages, and all the tests are not conclusive."

"Even so, it offers a ray of hope, doesn't it?"

He nodded. "The article said the berry juice is not a cure-all for every heart condition, but in weak hearts with capillary congestion, it's been proven to have great benefit."

"Will you try some of this extract on my father?"

"As soon as I get back to my office, I'll see about getting some hawthorn berries. Then I'll ask my nurse to pulverize them and make a tea."

"Thank you, Doctor. I hope this is the miracle I've been praying for."

As William came up the walk in front of the Nelsons' place, he could hear Bristle Face barking in the backyard. He was tempted to go around and greet the dog but figured he'd better make his call on Betsy's father first. Hiram hadn't been in church yesterday, and when Betsy said she'd left her father asleep in his chair, William had become concerned and decided to visit.

Just as he walked up the porch steps, the front door opened and Dr. McGrath stepped out. "Good afternoon, Reverend. I'm sorry I missed church yesterday, but I had a baby to deliver."

"One of the women at church told me that Mae Gates had gone into labor. Did the delivery go well?"

"Mae had a healthy baby boy. Her husband, Andy, said he thought his son might make a good preacher someday because he's got such a good set of lungs." The doctor chuckled. "Andy said he could hear the lad squalling all through the house."

William smiled, then motioned toward the house. "How's Hiram doing? I assume you were making a call on him."

"Yes, and I'm sorry to say that he's not doing well. His heart seems weaker today than it has on any of my previous visits."

"I'm sorry to hear that."

"I plan to try a new remedy, but a good dose of prayer wouldn't hurt either."

William nodded. "That's what I've come for. That and to offer some encouraging words to Hiram and his daughter."

"They'll appreciate that, I'm sure." Dr. McGrath lifted his hand in a wave and stepped off the porch.

William rapped on the front door, and moments later Betsy opened it. "I came to see your father. Is he up to some company?"

She opened the door wider, bidding him to enter. "He's very tired, but I'm sure he'll be pleased to see you."

William followed her inside. "Dr. McGrath mentioned something about a new medication he hopes to try on your father."

She nodded. "It's a tea made with hawthorn berries. The doctor read about it in a medical journal." Betsy's smile appeared hopeful. "Papa still needs a lot of prayer though."

"I've been praying for him and will continue to do so." William touched Betsy's shoulder. "I'll try to come by more often, and if you ever need anything, please don't hesitate to ask."

She paused outside her father's bedroom door and leaned against the wall. "Actually, there is something I've been meaning to ask you."

"What's that?"

"I was wondering if you might speak to some of the men from church about the possibility of putting a fence around our yard so I won't have to keep tying Bristle Face to a tree." Betsy grimaced. "That animal seems determined to break free and run over to the parsonage, and I'm sure it's become quite a nuisance for you."

William thought about the last time the dog had shown up at his door. Mrs. Bevens had threatened to chase him away with a broom. "I'm sure some of the men would be willing to build a fence," he said to Betsy. "I'll be happy to help out, too."

"Thank you." Betsy released a sigh. "I have one more favor to ask."

"What's that?"

"It's about my Sunday school class."

"I heard that it went quite well on Sunday. The McDougal girls told me they liked your puppets."

Betsy nodded. "I enjoyed teaching them, but with Papa taking a turn for the worse, I'm not sure I'll be able to continue teaching. I was hoping you might find someone else to take the class and maybe play the organ, too."

"I'm sure some of the women from church would be glad to sit with your father while you're teaching."

Betsy nibbled on her lower lip as she stared at the floor.

"Your help is much appreciated, and everyone at church benefits from your musical talents." He took a step forward. "I don't think it would be good for you to stay cooped up in the house all the time, and I'm sure your father would agree with me on that."

She lifted her gaze to meet his, and he noticed tears in her eyes. "I. . .I guess maybe I should take one week at a time and see how it goes."

William nodded. "Is there anything else you wish to discuss before I see your father?"

"That was all."

He turned toward her father's room and grasped the doorknob.

"Wait. There is one more thing."

He pivoted back around. "What is it, Betsy?"

"Please don't say anything to Papa about the hawthorn berry tea Dr. McGrath wants to try. I don't want to get his hopes up."

William shook his head. "Of course not. I'll merely offer some words of encouragement and pray with him."

"Thank you, Pastor William."

Chapter 12

*B*etsy bent over the washtub she'd set up on the back porch and grabbed a pair of overalls. It was time to do laundry again. Today she had her and Papa's clothes to do, as well as some from the boatmen. She'd been getting more business lately, which was a good thing because she needed the money. The washing and mending, however, kept her busier than ever, leaving less time to spend with her father.

For the last few weeks some of the women from church had taken turns relieving Betsy so she could teach Sunday school, play the organ during church, and go shopping whenever it was needed. During those weeks Dr. McGrath had been giving Betsy's father a dose of hawthorn berry tea every day, and they were waiting to see if it helped his heart any.

A fence had been put up around their backyard as well. Since Ben Hanson owned the house Betsy and her father lived in, he'd agreed to pay for the needed supplies. Several of the men from church, including Pastor William and Mike Cooper, had been involved in building the fence. Bristle Face was now safe and secure, and he couldn't make a pest of himself by going over to the parsonage and bothering Mrs. Bevens or the pastor anymore.

At the moment, the dog was sleeping on the porch, but when he let out a noisy yap, Betsy spotted Harriet Miller coming up the walk, carrying a wicker basket.

"I brought lunch over for you and your father," Harriet said once she'd reached the gate. "Would you like me to hand it over the fence, or should I come into the yard?"

Betsy dropped a just-washed pair of trousers into the rinse bucket and straightened. "If you'd like to go around front, I'll meet you there. If you come into the backyard, you'll have to deal with Bristle Face, which probably won't be pleasant."

Harriet's eyebrows lifted, and a blotch of pink erupted on her cheeks. "Oh dear, does the animal bite?"

"To my knowledge, Bristle Face has never bitten anyone, but he does like to jump up, and I'm sure you wouldn't appreciate his dirty paw prints all over your clean skirt."

Harriet nodded. "I'll head around front."

A few minutes later Betsy joined Harriet on the front porch. "It was kind of you to bring us a meal," she said, taking the basket from the elderly woman. "Would you care to come inside and say hello to my father while you're here?"

"Is he feeling up to company today?"

"I think so. He was relaxing on the sofa when I went outside to do the laundry, but I'm sure he would enjoy a visit from you."

Harriet smiled. "I'll go in to see him in a few minutes, but first, I'd like to have a little chat with you, if you have the time."

Betsy motioned to the two wicker chairs sitting near the door. When they were both seated, she placed the wicker basket on the porch by her chair. "Was there anything in particular you wished to speak with me about?"

"As a matter of fact, there is." Harriet smoothed the wrinkles in her long, gray skirt. "I've been meeting with some of the other women from church on Monday mornings, so we can pray, study our Bibles, and discuss the needs of our congregation."

"There seems to be many needs among us these days," Betsy said with a nod.

"You're so right, and one of the needs we've been praying about is a husband for you."

Betsy's mouth dropped open. "What?"

Harriet reached over and took hold of Betsy's hand.

"Look how red and wrinkled your skin has become since you started taking in washing. And I saw the way you grimaced in pain when you stood up from that washtub earlier." She clicked her tongue. "If you had a husband to provide for your needs, you wouldn't have to slave over a hot tub of water in order to earn money."

Betsy gripped the arms of her chair until her fingers dug into the wicker. "Are all the women in your group praying that I find a husband?"

Harriet nodded. "Most of us have attended the community church for a good many years, and we've known you since you were a little girl."

"That's true, but—"

"What about our handsome young preacher?"

"What about him?"

"I think you and Pastor William would make the perfect match."

"Oh, I don't believe—"

Harriet patted Betsy's hand in a motherly fashion. "Several of us think you would make a good minister's wife. After all, you've grown up in the ministry and know what's expected of a pastor and his family. Your musical abilities are certainly a plus, too."

Betsy swallowed hard. "Have I said or done anything to make you believe I've set my cap for the preacher?"

Harriet blinked. "Why, no, dear. I just think that the two of you are well suited, and—"

Betsy shook her head. "I'm not looking for a husband, Harriet."

"Haven't you noticed how kind and caring the pastor seems to be? He's such a handsome man, don't you think?"

Betsy didn't know how to respond. She had noticed how handsome the pastor was, and if she were still the old flirtatious Betsy, she might be tempted to let her interest in the man be known. But she had changed and would not throw herself at any man, no matter how much he might interest her. If God ever decided that she should have a husband, then He would have to cause that man to make the first move.

William couldn't get over all the invitations he'd recently received to share lunches and suppers with various people from his congregation. Yet here he was, stepping into another house for a noon meal. It was the third invitation in two days. Mrs. Bevens had been invited, too, but as usual she'd declined.

"Fred and I are so glad you could join us for lunch today," Doris Brown said as she led William into her roomy kitchen. "Why, when I told Fred you were coming over to eat, he said, 'I'll just knock over a chicken or two, and you can get out some flour doin's, and then we'll feed that new pastor of ours some tasty chicken fixin's.'" She offered William a wide grin and pointed to the table. "Fred's upstairs changing out of his dirty work clothes, but he'll be down soon, so why don't you pull up a chair and make yourself comfortable?"

William smiled and took the chair closest to him.

"Too bad your housekeeper couldn't have come over," Doris said. "She's not such a friendly type, is she?"

"What makes you think that?"

"Some of us women have been having ourselves a little Bible study on Monday mornings, and when I saw Mrs. Bevens at church a couple of Sundays ago, I asked if she'd like to join us."

"I see." William didn't bother to ask what reply his housekeeper had given, because he already knew Mrs. Bevens had declined the invitation. The snooty woman had mentioned that she didn't care much for people like Doris Brown, a plain, simple woman, lacking in education and social graces.

"I haven't been able to figure out if your housekeeper is stuck on herself or is just shy around folks she don't know so well." Doris reached around William to pour water into his glass. "The lady doesn't say much, and some of the women from church think she seems kind of hoity-toity, which makes no sense, seeing as to how she's workin' as your housekeeper and all."

William grimaced. Hoity-toity. That was exactly the impression Mrs. Bevens left with people.

Doris pulled out a chair on the other side of the table and

sat down, apparently in no hurry to get lunch on the table. "Can you tell me why Mrs. Bevens keeps her distance?"

William drew in a deep breath and released it quickly. "I've known Mrs. Bevens since I was a boy—when she was my nanny. It's my understanding that her father was once a successful businessman, but soon after his wife died, he started drinking and lost all his assets."

"Assets?"

"All his business holdings—his money."

"I see."

"So Mrs. Bevens, being an only child, was sent away to live with her old maid aunt because her father could no longer care for her." William paused. He hoped he wasn't speaking out of turn or that the information would appear to be gossip. But Doris had asked a direct question, and he felt she deserved an honest answer.

"Do you think Mrs. Bevens might've become bitter 'cause her daddy was a louse?" Doris leaned forward with her elbows on the table and blinked her eyelashes several times.

William shrugged. "Maybe so, but it's not my place to judge. I've probably spoken out of turn by telling you what I have about Mrs. Bevens."

"I'm glad you shared what you did 'cause it helps me understand the woman a little better." Doris pushed away from the table and lumbered over to the stove. She opened the oven door and peeked inside. "Chicken looks brown enough now, so we can eat as soon as my man shows up."

"If it tastes half as good as it smells, I'm sure I'll be in for a treat."

"Oh, it will—I can guarantee that," Doris's husband, Fred, said as he sauntered into the room with a towel slung over his shoulder. He stepped up beside his wife and planted a noisy kiss on her cheek. "My Doris is the best cook in the whole state of Pennsylvania."

"I think we have a church full of good cooks." William patted his stomach. "I've eaten several meals prepared by the ladies already, and I enjoyed every one."

Fred plodded over to the table and pulled out a chair. "Know what I think you need, Preacher?"

William opened his mouth to respond, but Doris cut him off. "He needs a wife, that's what he needs."

Fred's bald head bobbed up and down. "That's just what I was gonna say. It ain't good for a preacher man to be single."

Doris placed a platter full of chicken on the table and patted William on the back. "I know exactly who the perfect wife for you would be."

William fiddled with the knife beside his plate as his face heated up. Was everyone in the church determined to see him married?

"It's Frank Andrews's daughter, Hortence, huh?" Fred jiggled his bushy eyebrows and gave William a silly grin. "I've seen the way that little gal looks at you on Sunday mornings."

William's ears burned, and a trickle of sweat rolled down his forehead.

"Oh no, Fred," Doris said as she set a bowl of mashed potatoes in front of William. "I think Betsy Nelson would be more suitable as a pastor's wife, don't you?"

William cringed. *I think it's time for me to nip this talk of marriage in the bud.* This Sunday, before he began his sermon, he would let everyone in the congregation know that he was perfectly happy being single and that he planned to stay that way.

Chapter 13

On Sunday morning as William stepped into the pulpit, he reminded himself what his first announcement should be. His only concern was in choosing the right words. He didn't want to hurt anyone's feelings, yet he couldn't allow the folks who had been trying to play matchmaker to continue inviting him to dinner with the hope of getting him married off to their daughters.

He placed his Bible on the pulpit, collected his thoughts as best he could, and smiled at the congregation. "Good morning. This is the day that the Lord hath made."

Several *amen*s went up around the room, and many people nodded their heads in agreement.

"I. . .uh. . .have an announcement to make." William loosened his tie a notch and swallowed around the constriction in his throat. Everyone wore expectant looks, even Betsy, who sat at the organ with her hymnbook in her hands. Would he embarrass someone if he said this in front of the entire congregation? He didn't want to cause hard feelings or draw attention to anyone in particular. Maybe it would be better if he spoke one-on-one to the individuals who were determined to play matchmaker, rather than announcing to the whole group that he was a confirmed bachelor.

William gripped the edge of the pulpit for support. Why did the room feel so hot all of a sudden? The windows were open, so a breeze must be coming in. These people were expecting him to make an announcement, so if he wasn't going to say what was on his mind, then he needed to come up with something else to say.

He cleared his throat a couple of times. "My. . .uh. . . announcement this morning is that. . .uh. . . ."

"What's the matter, Preacher? Are you gonna chew us out because we've done somethin' wrong?" Abe Rawlings, one of the few canalers who came to church whenever his boat passed through the area, shouted from the back of the room.

William shook his head, feeling more frustrated than ever. He needed to think of something to announce, and it had better be quick. "No one has done anything wrong. I just wanted to announce that—" An idea suddenly popped into his head, and he practically shouted out the rest of his sentence. "Next Sunday, after the worship service is over, I want to conduct another service down by the canal, and a. . .a picnic will follow."

Several heads bobbed up and down, and smiles spread across most of the people's faces.

"Shortly after I came here, it was brought to my attention that the boatmen might enjoy some singing and preaching down at the canal, where their boats are tied up for their day of rest." He glanced over at Betsy, knowing this had been her idea, and added, "I hope all of you will come and be part of this special service."

"You can count on me, Pastor."

"I'll be there."

"Yeah, me, too."

"A picnic sounds like fun."

Everyone seemed to be talking at once, and William rapped his knuckles on the edge of the pulpit to get their attention. "Perhaps some of you ladies can get together and discuss what you might want to bring for the picnic. I think it would be nice if each family brought enough food to share with some of the canalers, don't you?"

Several heads nodded in agreement, and a couple of women started whispering to those who sat near them.

William tapped on the pulpit again. "Rather than taking time to discuss the details of the picnic right now, I think it would be better if we waited until after church is over."

"The preacher man's right!" Abe hollered. "We came here to sing God's praises and hear His Word, not talk about food!"

Everyone quieted, and William looked over at Betsy again. "Perhaps you could meet with me for a few minutes after church today, along with any others who might want to sing a special song or play a musical instrument during our canal service."

Betsy nodded and smiled.

When church was over and the final prayer had been said, Betsy stood near the organ, waiting for the pastor to finish greeting the people so he could meet with her and any others who might want to contribute to the music next Sunday during the canal service. She was pleased that Pastor William had decided to hold church there. It had meant a lot to the boatmen whenever Papa walked the canal to hand out Bible verses or conducted a Sunday service in the grassy area near the towpath. Many men, including Kelly and Sarah's father, Amos McGregor, had found a personal relationship with the Lord because of those informal meetings. Now whenever Amos and his wife were near Walnutport on a Saturday evening, they would tie up for the night and come to church on Sunday morning. Betsy knew how pleased Kelly and Sarah were when their folks were able to be in church, and the look of pride on Dorrie McGregor's face as she sat on a pew, holding one of her grandchildren in her lap, was a joy to behold.

"Excuse me," Ruby Miller said as she stepped up beside Betsy, "but I was wondering if I might speak to you a minute."

Betsy nodded. "Of course. Were you wanting to sing a special song at our canal service next Sunday?"

Ruby's face turned pink, and she fanned her face with her hands. "Oh my, no. I'd scare folks away if I tried to sing a solo."

Betsy smiled at the middle-aged woman and gently squeezed her arm. "You wouldn't have to sing a solo. You could do a duet with me or someone else from the congregation."

Ruby shook her head. "My husband says I squawk like a chicken whenever I sing, so I wouldn't think of embarrassing anyone by asking them to do a duet with me."

"So what did you wish to speak with me about?"

Ruby leaned closer to Betsy and whispered, "I was hoping you and your father might come to supper at our place one night next week."

"It's nice of you to ask, but I don't think Papa's up to going anywhere right now." Betsy gestured to the empty pews. "You've probably noticed he hasn't been in church for the last couple of weeks."

Ruby nodded. "I'm sorry he's not doing any better. We're

all praying for him, you know."

"We appreciate that."

"Would your father be okay with you coming to dinner without him? I could ask someone to sit with him while you're gone, if that would help." Ruby touched Betsy's shoulder. "You really do need a break once in a while."

"I'll think about it and let you know." Betsy offered Ruby what she hoped was a pleasant smile.

"I'll stop by your house on Tuesday for an answer, and if you decide to accept my invitation, we'll have you over for supper on Friday evening."

Ruby walked away, and a few minutes later Pastor William showed up. "Was Ruby talking to you about the music for our canal service next week?"

Betsy shook her head. "She had something else on her mind."

"I see. Well, I hope you'll be able to take part in the services. I would like it if you brought your zither along to accompany the songs."

"As long as my father isn't any worse and I can find someone to spend the afternoon with him, I'll be there," Betsy said with a nod.

"It would be wonderful if he felt up to going along that day."

"Yes, it would."

"Does the doctor think the new treatment is helping at all?"

Betsy shrugged. "He's not sure. There are days when Papa seems a bit stronger and doesn't have as much chest pain, but other days he can barely walk across the room without having to stop every few seconds to catch his breath."

"The last time I spoke with your father, he informed me that he's ready to die if the Lord chooses to take him home rather than heal his heart."

A shiver started at the base of Betsy's neck and ran all the way down her spine. She could hardly think about Papa dying, much less speak the words.

"I apologize if I've spoken out of turn. I can see that you're shaken." Pastor William nodded toward the organ bench. "Would you like to sit awhile?"

"I'm fine." Betsy grabbed the hymnbook from the end of the organ where she had placed it after the service. "Should we pick some songs for next Sunday now?"

"Yes. Yes, of course."

Chapter 14

I'm sorry you couldn't come over to our place for supper last week," Ruby said to Betsy as they both pulled their buckboards into a clearing near the section of the canal closest to the lock tender's house.

Betsy glanced over at her father, who sat in the seat beside her. "Papa wasn't feeling well that night, and—"

"I tried to get her to go, but my daughter can be so stubborn sometimes." Papa nodded at Betsy. "I love you and appreciate your dedication, but you worry about me too much."

Betsy couldn't argue with that. She did worry about her father and wanted him to get well so they could spend more time together.

"I'm glad you're feeling up to attending our church service and picnic at the canal today," Ruby said. "Sure wish my husband would have been able to come."

"Is Clem sick?" Betsy asked. "I didn't see him at our service in town."

"He's not sick, but yesterday morning that determined man put a kink in his back when he tried to move a huge rock in our backyard." Ruby pursed her lips. "He was still hurtin' this morning and didn't want to get out of bed. Said I should go to church without him."

"Clem should have asked some of the men from church to help him move that rock," Betsy's father put in. "That's how we got our fence put up. Isn't that right, Betsy?"

She nodded and reached over to touch his hand. "Are you sure you're up to this outing today?"

He squeezed her fingers. "I'm fine, and I wouldn't have missed seeing my canal friends here—not to mention sampling some of the tasty food the ladies from church have brought along to share."

"I baked some apple pies," Ruby said. "That's always been a favorite of yours."

He grinned and patted his stomach. "Yes, Ruby, I do love your sweet apple pies."

Betsy smiled. The fact that Papa seemed so pleased gave her hope that he might be feeling better. If God provided a miracle and healed Papa's heart, he might be able to start preaching again. Of course, now there was a new pastor standing in his pulpit, so either William would have to leave or Papa would need to look for some other church to pastor. The thought of them moving away from Walnutport didn't set well with Betsy, and thinking about the new pastor leaving wasn't much better. Betsy wouldn't have admitted it to anyone, but in the short time Pastor William had been in town, she'd become quite fond of him. He seemed kind, caring, and smart, and he was extremely good-looking. She was sure he would make a fine husband.

Betsy's shoulders tensed as a pain shot up her neck, and her musings came to a halt. What on earth had she been thinking? Friendship was all she could offer right now, and she was sure the pastor saw her only as a friend as well.

"Shall we climb down from the buckboard and join the others?" Papa asked.

Betsy nodded. "Let me put a blanket on the grass so you'll have a comfortable place to sit, and then I'll come back to the buckboard to get you."

"I'm not an invalid, Betsy. And I don't plan to sit on a blanket all day."

Betsy knew her father's words weren't meant to be harsh, but she felt the sting of them nonetheless. "I just don't want you overdoing it. This is the first day in a long while that you've been outside the house."

He patted her arm. "I'll be fine."

A short time later as Betsy, her father, and Ruby headed for the canal, she spotted Mike and Kelly along with their two children: Anna, who was four, and Marcus, who had just turned two.

"Pastor Nelson, it's so good to see you," Mike said, taking Betsy's father by the arm.

"I wouldn't have missed coming here today for anything," Papa replied. The two men wandered off, Ruby joined Freda Hanson, who stood nearby, and Betsy followed Kelly and her children across the grass.

"I think I'm going to set out my blanket and picnic basket before the service begins," Kelly said. "That way we'll be sure to have a good place to sit when it's time to eat."

Betsy nodded. "Guess I'll do the same."

The children sat on the grass and watched as Kelly and Betsy spread out their blankets. They'd just gotten everything situated when Kelly's mother and sister—Dorrie and Sarah—showed up. Sarah's three children—Sam Jr., age six; Willis, who was four; and two-year-old Helen—tagged along behind them.

Kelly's children scurried over to their grandmother, and she gave them each a hug. "I'm so glad the new pastor has decided to hold services down here by the canal." She smiled at Betsy. "Since your father retired from preaching, those of us who spend most of the week on our boats have missed this time of singing, Bible teaching, and fellowship."

"That's right," Sarah said with a nod. "Even though my family usually makes it to church in town most Sundays, we've always enjoyed the services held here along the water."

"Mike and I have enjoyed that, too," Kelly agreed.

"Betsy, did you bring your zither?" Dorrie asked.

Betsy nodded and pointed to the leather case she'd set on one end of the blanket. "I'm just waiting for our pastor to arrive."

Sarah glanced at the group of people who had already congregated. "I would think he would have been here by now. I hope he didn't change his mind about holding the service down here."

"I'm sure Pastor William is coming," Betsy said. "He helped me pick out the songs we're going to sing today, and he seemed excited about the opportunity to preach to the boatmen."

Kelly poked Betsy gently on the arm and motioned to the left. "Here he comes now, and he's got his housekeeper with him."

William was amazed at how many people had gathered along the grassy banks near the canal. He recognized several from church, but lots of faces were new to him.

"I don't see why you insisted that I be here for this," Mrs. Bevens said through tight lips as she tromped through the tall grass beside him. "I attended services at your church this morning; that ought to be good enough."

"I thought you might use this time as an opportunity to

get to know the people in the community a little better," he said, patting her arm. "It's a warm, sunny afternoon with not much humidity, and it's the perfect day for a picnic."

"Perfect for the ants and buzzing insects maybe." Mrs. Bevens lifted the edge of her long, gray skirt and frowned. "If I get grass stains on my dress, it will be your fault."

William clenched his teeth and kept on walking. He was nervous enough about conducting his first outdoor service, and he didn't need Mrs. Bevens's negative attitude to put a damper on things. He spotted Betsy standing beside Kelly and her sister and was relieved to see that she'd brought her zither along.

"Should we begin with some singing?" he asked, moving away from Mrs. Bevens and stepping up to Betsy.

She nodded. "That's the way Papa always began his services." She motioned to a log lying a few feet from the towpath. Her father was sitting there with Mike Cooper on one side of him and Sam Turner on the other side.

"I'm glad your father could make it. I didn't see him in church this morning, so I assumed he wasn't feeling well."

"He says he's feeling better today, but he knew it would be too long of a day if he went to church in town and came here, too." Betsy smiled. "So he chose to attend this service and the picnic that will follow."

"Our dad's here today, too," Sarah put in.

"That's right. Preacher Nelson led Papa to the Lord some time ago," Kelly added. "He's not as comfortable comin' into town to the fancy church building, but ever since he accepted Christ as his Savior, Papa has enjoyed the services held along the canal."

"That's good to hear. If things go well today, I'll try to hold services down here on a regular basis."

Kelly and Sarah smiled, and Betsy fairly beamed. "I'm ready to get started with the singing whenever you are, Pastor," she said.

William moved over to the crowd of people and lifted his hands. "Good afternoon. For those of you who haven't met me yet, I'm Pastor William Covington, and I'm pleased to see so many of you here today."

There were several *amen*s, a few people snickered, and a couple of the canalers shouted, "Nice to meet ya, Preacher!"

William's cheeks warmed, and he knew it wasn't from the summer sun. The people at the church he'd attended in Buffalo were so formal and stuffy compared to these plain, simple folks who weren't afraid to show enthusiasm or say whatever was on their mind. Nothing William had learned in seminary had prepared him for preaching to a group of unpretentious, uneducated canalers, but he was ready and willing to do the Lord's work, no matter what it took.

William opened the service with a word of prayer then announced the first song they would sing: "Shall We Gather at the River?" He nodded at Betsy, and she began to strum her zither. Everyone's voices blended together as they sang out, "Shall we gather at the river, where bright angel feet have trod, with its crystal tide forever flowing by the throne of God?'"

William was pleased to see a look of joy on the people's faces, as they lifted their heads toward the sky and sang with gusto. He led them in two more songs, "What a Friend We Have in Jesus" and "Wonderful Words of Life," and was about to launch into his sermon when a voice from the crowd shouted, "I would like it if we sang, 'I Feel Like Traveling On'!"

William turned to see Hiram Nelson walking toward him, his face fairly glowing and his eyes shimmering with tears. "Of course we can sing that song. Would you like to lead us, Rev. Nelson?"

Hiram nodded, and in a surprisingly steady voice he began, "'My heavenly home is bright and fair. I feel like traveling on. Nor pain nor death can enter there. I feel like traveling on.'" He motioned to the crowd, and they joined him on the chorus: "'Yes, I feel like traveling on. I feel like traveling on. My heavenly home is bright and fair. I feel like traveling on.'"

When the song ended, Rev. Nelson lifted his hands and looked upward. "I'm ready to go home whenever You're ready to take me, Lord!"

Chapter 15

*B*etsy didn't know how she'd managed to sit through Pastor William's message when the singing ended, because after Papa's song and him telling God that he was ready to go home to be with Him, she felt numb. Just this morning Papa had told her that he was feeling better. Yet his choice of song and the prayer that followed made it clear that he was ready to die.

Papa sat on the blanket beside her now, smiling and licking his lips as he ate a chicken wing he'd pulled from the covered dish Betsy had taken from their picnic basket a few minutes ago. Didn't he realize how much he'd upset her with that song and prayer?

"This is sure tasty," he said with a smile. "You're going to make some man a mighty fine wife some day."

Betsy shook her head. "I'm an old maid, Papa, and I'm quite likely to stay one."

"You never know what the future holds." He glanced over at her half-eaten plate of food and frowned. "You've barely touched a thing. I can't eat all this by myself, you know."

She shrugged, wishing she felt free to tell her father all the things that were on her mind. "I'm not so hungry right now."

His eyebrows furrowed. "How come? Are you feeling sick?"

"No, I'm not sick."

"That's good to hear." Papa took another bite of chicken and wiped his mouth on the napkin she'd just handed him. "That young pastor sure preached a good sermon on forgiveness this afternoon, didn't he?"

Betsy shifted uncomfortably on the blanket. "I'm. . . uh. . .glad Pastor William decided to hold services down here." She didn't want to admit that she hadn't heard more than a few words of the pastor's message. "Several of the boatmen have told me how much they've missed the meetings you used to hold along the canal."

Her father nodded and reached for the cup of water Betsy had placed on the lid of the picnic basket. "I'm pleased to see such a good turnout, and I'm hoping Pastor William will continue to hold services here on a regular basis."

"I'm sure he will, as long as the weather cooperates."

Betsy sighed and set her plate aside.

He cast her a furtive glance. "Are you sure you're all right?"

She nodded and offered him what she hoped was a reassuring smile.

"I can tell by the wrinkles in your forehead that something is bothering you, so you may as well tell me what it is."

Betsy drew in a deep breath and released it quickly, glancing around to be sure no one sitting nearby was listening. "I'm worried about you, Papa."

"Now, Betsy, you know what the Bible says about worry. 'Therefore I say unto you, Take no thought for your life, what ye shall eat, or what ye shall drink; nor yet for your body, what ye shall put on. Is not the life more than meat, and the body than raiment?' Matthew 6:25."

Betsy grimaced. "I'm not worried about what I shall eat or wear, Papa. After hearing that song you sang earlier and listening to your prayer, I became worried that you might have given up on life and were preparing to die."

"We're all going to die sometime." Papa reached over and patted her hand. "You must remember that no matter what happens in the days ahead, my life is in God's hands."

Betsy opened her mouth to comment, but he rushed on. "No one but God knows what the future holds, but we do know that our heavenly Father holds the future, so let us remember to be loyal to Him and leave our destiny in His hands."

Betsy swallowed hard, trying to dislodge the lump that had formed in her throat. "I know, Papa, and I'll try not to worry."

"That's my girl," he said with a wink. "Now why don't you let your old papa take a nap while you visit with some of your friends?"

Betsy didn't feel like visiting with anyone right now, but because she knew her father needed to rest, she gathered up their plates and leftover food, placed them inside the picnic basket, and stood. Smoothing the wrinkles in her long, green skirt, she smiled down at him. "I'll come back in half an hour to check on you."

He reclined on the blanket, placing both hands behind his head. "No need to worry about me. I'll be fine."

———— ❋ ————

"I'm going over to talk with Rev. Nelson for a bit," William said to Mrs. Bevens as she began putting away their leftover picnic food. "While I'm gone, why don't you try to get to know some of the ladies here a little better?"

Mrs. Bevens's mouth drooped at the corners. "I'd rather be alone. Maybe I will take a walk along the canal."

He released a frustrated groan. "Suit yourself, but you'll never feel at home in Walnutport unless you learn to mingle."

She pursed her lips and kept piling things into the wicker basket.

William rose from the blanket. "Have a nice walk, Mrs. Bevens."

A short time later he found Hiram Nelson lying under the shade of a leafy maple tree. The man's eyes were closed, and his steady, even breathing indicated that he must be sleeping. William was about to walk away, when the reverend said, "Don't run off. I'd like to talk to you."

William jumped. "I thought you were sleeping."

"Nope. Just resting my eyes." Hiram sat up and motioned William over to the blanket. "Have a seat, and we can visit awhile."

"Are you sure I'm not interrupting your nap?"

"I can sleep any old time." He chuckled. "To tell you the truth, I only said I wanted to take a nap so my daughter would feel free to leave my side and spend some time with her friends."

William glanced across the grassy area near the towpath and spotted Betsy sitting on a blanket beside Kelly and her sister, Sarah. "A couple of women from church have mentioned to me that Betsy doesn't socialize much."

"That's because she spends all her time washing and mending clothes for the canalers and, of course, tending to my needs."

"Betsy takes good care of you. It's obvious that she loves you very much."

"And I love her." Hiram pointed to the towpath where Mrs. Bevens walked alone. "Your housekeeper takes care of your basic needs, too, but she'll never take the place of a wife."

William's mouth dropped open. Surely Rev. Nelson wasn't in on the plot to see him married off, too.

"I wouldn't be so bold as to try and pick a wife for you," Hiram continued, "but I do think if you found the right helpmate it would benefit your ministry."

"But—but you have no wife, and from what I've heard, you got along just fine," William sputtered.

Hiram pulled his fingers through his thinning brown hair. "I was widowed when Betsy was a young girl, and many people thought I should find another wife."

"But you stayed single and did okay in your ministry. Am I right about that?"

Hiram nodded. "Yes, but that was because I never found a woman I could love as much as Betsy's mother. Abigail was a special lady, and she made me feel complete in so many. . ." His voice trailed off, as he stared into space.

William sat there a few seconds, allowing Hiram the privilege of reminiscing. After a few minutes he touched the man's arm. "I suppose I should let you get back to your nap. Unless there was more you wanted to say."

"Actually, there is one thing I'd like to mention."

"What's that?"

The older man cleared his throat. "This is. . .uh. . .a bit difficult for me to say, but I get the feeling that you might be putting a safe distance between you and your flock."

He moistened his lips with the tip of his tongue. "At first I thought it was because you thought you were better than them, since you're more educated and all."

A shock wave spiraled through William, but before he could offer a retort, Hiram added, "Now that I've gotten to know you better, I no longer believe that is true. I think the real reason you're keeping your distance is because you've been hurt by someone—perhaps a woman."

William clasped his hands together so hard that two of his knuckles popped. "I don't see what this has to do with anything."

Hiram laid a hand on William's shoulder. "If you want your ministry in Walnutport to succeed, then you're going to have to do more than preach a good sermon. You'll need to become part of the congregation—bring yourself down to their level: laugh with them, cry with them, become one of them. You must ask God to help you set your fears aside and become vulnerable enough to love and be loved by these people—and maybe by some special woman."

William blinked rapidly. "I don't know what to say."

"Just say you'll think about what I've said and also pray about it."

"Yes. Yes, of course I will." William rose. "You look tired, and I probably should mingle a bit and get to know some of the boatmen."

Hiram smiled, and William noticed the moisture clinging to the man's eyelashes. "Good for you, Pastor. Good for you."

As William started to walk away, two young boys raced past, shouting and tossing a ball back and forth as they zigzagged around the blankets where people sat visiting. "It's a wonder those two don't bump into someone," he muttered.

The boys kept running past the grassy area and onto the towpath. One threw the ball, and the other ran ahead to catch it, laughing and hollering as he went. William caught sight of his housekeeper again, standing along the edge of the canal, apparently deep in thought. He was about to call out a warning that a ball might be coming her way when the sphere of white whizzed through the air and smacked Mrs. Bevens on the back. She let out a muffled grunt and tumbled into the canal.

William rushed toward the water, but Harvey Collins, one of the canalers, jumped in first. William stood on the bank of the canal, watching as Mrs. Bevens flailed about, hollering, "I'm drowning!" while poor old Harvey struggled to drag her to shore.

Mrs. Bevens came out of the water, looking like a soggy scarecrow, and the unpleasant words she spewed told William she saw the incident as anything but funny. The finicky woman's hair had come loose from its perfect bun and stuck out in odd directions. Her stylish dress that had once been neatly pressed and stiffly starched at the collar clung to her body like it had been soaked with glue.

"Who did this to me?" Mrs. Bevens bellowed, as she spit

water out of her mouth and stumbled onto shore. "I knew I should not have come here today!"

"That dunk in the canal sure took the wind out of your snooty sails, didn't it?" Harvey chuckled as he squeezed water out of his own sopping clothes.

"Maybe what she needed was a good lesson in humility!" one of the other canalers called.

William couldn't argue with that. Mrs. Bevens did need to be taught a lesson, but he couldn't help feeling sorry for her as she spluttered away. Even Mrs. Bevens didn't deserve this kind of embarrassment.

Betsy rushed forward with a quilt and wrapped it around Mrs. Bevens's trembling shoulders. Not a word of thanks came from the woman's quivering lips—not to Betsy for the quilt or to Harvey for saving her life. Mrs. Bevens needed a lot of prayer, and William knew that was one thing he could do without her scolding him for it. He stepped forward and offered his arm. "I think it's time we went home, don't you?"

She gave a curt nod then tromped off toward William's buggy.

He nodded at Betsy and then at Harvey. "Thank you both for your kindness."

Chapter 16

I'll be on the back porch, washing some clothes, if you need me for anything," Betsy told her father as she positioned a small pillow behind his head, where he reclined on the sofa. He had come to the sitting room to read his Bible soon after breakfast, saying he wanted to spend time praying and meditating over God's Word.

I need to do that more often, too, Betsy thought, bending over to kiss his forehead.

"Don't work too hard, daughter. And always remember that I love you and wish you nothing but God's best."

"I love you, too, Papa." Betsy hurried out to the porch, anxious to get the washing out of the way so she could spend time with her father. She had convinced herself that if she cared for him properly, he would get well and things would be as they had been before his heart had started acting up. After seeing how well he'd done yesterday at the canal service, Betsy was beginning to believe that God might answer her prayers for a miracle.

Returning to the kitchen, Betsy hauled a kettle of hot water out to the porch, poured it into the washtub, added some lye soap, and dropped in one of the canalers' shirts. She reached into the hot, soapy water and dipped the shirt up and down several times, making sure it was sufficiently wet.

An image of Mrs. Bevens popped into her mind, and she bit back a chuckle. If she lived to be ninety, she didn't think she would ever forget seeing William's prim and proper housekeeper falling into the canal. Mrs. Bevens hadn't offered Harvey Collins any thanks at all for saving her life. For that matter, she hadn't thanked Betsy for the quilt she'd put around her shoulders.

A prick of conscience made Betsy shake her head. "It's not my place to judge Mrs. Bevens. Forgive me, Lord, for thinking such thoughts."

Betsy scrubbed the shirt against the washboard and gritted her teeth as she reflected on the way she used to be—self-centered and snobbish, always wanting her own way. She could have ended up just like Mrs. Bevens if she hadn't turned her life over to God and allowed Him to soften her heart.

She closed her eyes and offered up a heartfelt prayer. *Dear Lord, help me remember to set a good example to others and remind me whenever necessary that, but for Your grace, I could still be a snooty, selfish woman.*

Some time later, when all the clothes had been washed and hung on the line to dry, Betsy entered the kitchen. She filled a kettle with water and placed it on the stove with the intent of making her father his daily cup of hawthorn berry tea. While the water heated, she took a hunk of salt pork from the cooler, cut it into small pieces, and fried it in a pan to get the grease out, then she set it aside. She would add some potatoes, onion, tomatoes, and corn to the pot and then get some pork float cooking for their noon meal as soon as she had served Papa his tea.

Betsy placed a teacup on a wooden tray, filled it with water and the proper amount of the herb, and then headed for the sitting room. She stepped through the doorway, halted, and gasped. Papa lay facedown on the floor.

As William strolled down the sidewalk, prepared to make a few pastoral calls, he hummed his favorite hymn, "Where He Leads, I'll Follow," and thought about Sunday's service and the picnic that had followed. Most events during the day had encouraged his soul. He'd gotten to know several of the boatmen, become better acquainted with those who attended his church, had a pleasant conversation with Betsy's father, and filled his stomach with enough food to last him all week. The only sour note had been Mrs. Bevens's unplanned dip in the Lehigh Canal.

William couldn't help but feel sorry for the poor woman as he remembered how pathetic she'd looked when she came out of the water with porcupine hair and waterlogged clothes. The hoity-toity woman who'd gotten knocked into the canal had stepped onto dry land looking like an ordinary commoner. Unfortunately the incident hadn't done anything to soften Mrs. Bevens's heart.

I wish I could think of some way to get my dear housekeeper to move back to Buffalo, he thought ruefully. *Unless the Lord changes that frustrated woman's heart, she will never fit in here.*

Reminding himself that he needed to focus on something positive, William continued his trek down the street with a firm resolve. *I think I'll make my first call at the Nelsons' home and see how Hiram is doing.*

He had just turned onto Elm Street, when he almost collided with Betsy running at full speed. Her face looked pale, and her eyes were wide and full of fear.

"Betsy, what's wrong?" William clasped her shoulders.

"It–it's Papa. I was bringing him a cup of tea, and I f–found him lying on the floor. I couldn't get him to respond, and I'm afraid he might be—" Betsy choked on the words, and William instinctively drew her into his arms. "I've—I've got to get Dr. McGrath to come now. He needs to see Papa right away," she sobbed.

Realizing how shaken she was, he said, "I'll go with you to Dr. McGrath's."

Betsy pulled free from his embrace and darted down the street. William followed at a fast pace, reaching for Betsy's hand when he caught up to her. By the time they arrived at the doctor's office, Betsy could barely speak. "It's Papa. It's Papa. I think he's dead!" she gasped.

The doctor grabbed his black bag, said a few words to his nurse, and ushered them quickly out the door. "Let's take my carriage; it's around back." He nodded toward the back of the small building that served as his office.

When they stepped inside the Nelsons' home a short time later, William halted inside the door. Hiram lay on the sitting room floor, unmoving. Betsy rushed to her father's side. Dr. McGrath knelt next to her, opened his bag, and removed a stethoscope. "Help me turn him over, would you, Rev. Covington?"

William rushed across the room and dropped to his knees. Once they'd gotten Hiram turned onto his back, he could see that the man's face was deathly pale. There was no movement in his chest. William waited as the doctor placed the stethoscope over Hiram's heart so he could listen for a heartbeat.

Several minutes went by, which seemed like an eternity, then Dr. McGrath removed the stethoscope and placed his thumb over Hiram's wrist. He shook his head slowly as he looked over at Betsy. "There's no pulse, and I detected no heartbeat either. I'm sorry, but your father is dead."

Betsy sat there staring at her father. "Papa," she murmured.

William reached for her hand. "Your father's at peace now. He's gone home to be with Jesus."

Betsy blinked. Tears welled in her eyes, spilling onto her flushed cheeks. "Just yesterday Papa said he was feeling better." She squeezed her eyes shut. "But his song and prayer during the canal service were an indication that he knew he was going to die."

William winced, feeling her pain as though it were his own. Apparently Betsy's father had used the last of his strength to attend that service, and the song he'd sung and the prayer he'd prayed had been his final testimony.

"Lord, help Betsy in the days ahead," William prayed aloud. "Give her the strength and courage to go on." He gulped. The Rev. Hiram Nelson's funeral would be the first such service he'd ever conducted.

Chapter 17

*A*s Betsy stood near her father's coffin, she squeezed her eyes shut, willing herself not to break down during his graveside service. She'd held up fairly well during the service at the church, so she must maintain control of her emotions here. Despite her resolve, she wasn't sure how long she could hold out, for the pain in her heart was worse than any physical agony she'd ever endured. There seemed to be no answers to the questions filling her mind, and that only fueled her frustration. Why hadn't God healed Papa's heart? Why couldn't He have given them a few more years together?

"Dearly beloved, we have gathered today to pay our

final tribute and respects to the Rev. Hiram Nelson." Pastor William's deep voice broke into Betsy's thoughts, and her eyes snapped open.

I must not break down. I must remain strong.

"Forasmuch as the spirit of our departed loved one has returned to God, who gave it, we therefore tenderly commit his body to the grave." William paused long enough to open his Bible. "In John 14:1–3, we are told: 'Let not your heart be troubled: ye believe in God, believe also in me. In my Father's house are many mansions: if it were not so, I would have told you. I go to prepare a place for you. And if I go and prepare a place for you, I will come again, and receive you unto myself; that where I am, there ye may be also.'"

Papa's in heaven. That thought should have offered Betsy comfort, but she only felt grief.

"In John 11:25–26, Jesus said, 'I am the resurrection, and the life: he that believeth in me, though he were dead, yet shall he live: and whosoever liveth and believeth in me shall never die.'" William closed the Bible, and his gaze swept over the crowd of mourners. "May each of us find comfort in the knowledge that, while Hiram's body is dead, his soul lives on. Because this dedicated man believed in Jesus and accepted Him as his personal Savior, he now abides with the heavenly Father, where there are many mansions."

In spite of Betsy's resolve not to cry, tears flooded her eyes and streamed down her face, dripping onto the front of her black mourning dress. She felt all stirred up—as if her churning insides were as hot as coals. It was a comfort to know Papa no longer suffered and was now with Jesus, but oh, how she would miss him.

As Pastor William led the group in reciting the Lord's Prayer, Betsy pressed her lips together in an effort to keep from sobbing out loud. Instead of concentrating on the prayer, she thought about the funeral dinner Freda Hanson would be hosting at her house after the committal and wondered how she could get through the rest of the day.

———————❖———————

William didn't know how he'd made it through Hiram's funeral, but God had graciously given him the words he needed for the message he'd shared at the church and then at the cemetery. He hoped the words of condolence he'd offered to Hiram's grieving daughter had been helpful, but he felt there was more he should have said.

As the group of mourners entered the Hansons' house, William prayed that God would show him, as well as others in the church, how to comfort Betsy in the days ahead.

"You did a fine job conducting the funeral today," Mike said, handing William a cup of coffee and steering him toward one of the tables that had been set up in the living room.

Once he was seated, William took a tentative sip. Realizing the coffee was cool enough to drink, he gulped some down. "Thank you. As you may have guessed, this was the first funeral I've ever done, and I was a little nervous."

Mike thumped William lightly on the back. "It didn't show. You seemed to be in perfect control." He glanced across the room to where Betsy stood talking to Kelly. "Betsy seems to be holding up well, don't you think?"

William nodded but made no comment. Despite the fact that Betsy appeared to be doing all right, her eyes looked hollow and tired, like she hadn't slept much since her father's death.

"I wonder if now that her father's gone, Betsy will return to New York and her work with the Salvation Army."

William's hand jerked, and some of the coffee spilled onto the table. If Betsy left, who would play the organ on Sunday mornings? And what about the girls' Sunday school class she'd been teaching? "Has she said anything to you or your wife about leaving?"

"Well, no, but I just assumed—"

"Walnutport is her home, is it not?"

Mike nodded.

"I would think she would want to stay close to the place where her father is buried and where she has friends to offer comfort."

"Maybe she will." Mike smiled. "I guess the only way to know what plans she might make is to come right out and ask her. What do you think, Pastor?"

William set his cup down and reached up to loosen his

tie. "Are you suggesting that I ask what her plans are?"

"I don't see why not." Mike's head bobbed up and down. "You are her pastor, after all."

"Well, yes, that's true, but—"

"I didn't see your housekeeper at the funeral this morning," Clara Andrews interrupted as she plunked down beside William. "That was some tumble she took into the canal last Sunday. I hope she didn't come down with a cold because of it."

"Mrs. Bevens is fine. She's a little embarrassed by what happened, and I don't think she's ready to socialize with anyone yet," William replied.

"Humph!" Clara folded her arms across her ample chest and frowned. "A funeral service is hardly a social function. I would think she would have had the decency to offer her condolences to Rev. Nelson's grieving daughter."

William couldn't argue with that. He had told Mrs. Bevens the same thing this morning when she'd refused to accompany him to the funeral service. "I came to Walnutport to look out for your needs, not to socialize with the people in your congregation," Mrs. Bevens had said.

William figured that with Mrs. Bevens's dour attitude, it was better that she wasn't here today. He was sure she wouldn't have offered Betsy much comfort, and she might have said something rude or condescending.

He glanced across the room again and noticed that Kelly had moved away and Betsy now stood alone. "If you'll excuse me, Clara, I think I should see how Miss Nelson is doing."

Betsy was about to head into the kitchen to see if she could find something that would keep her hands busy, when Pastor William stepped up to her. "I was wondering if there's anything you might need—anything I can do for you."

She bit her bottom lip to stop the flow of tears. Why did it make her feel worse when someone offered help or sympathy? "I'll be fine," she replied, not really believing it. The truth was, Betsy didn't know if she could make it through the next minute, let alone the next hour, day, or week. The future looked bleak and frightening without Papa. She felt like a canal boat that had broken free from its towrope and had no purpose, no sense of direction, no haven of rest.

William touched her arm. "You don't have to go through this alone. The people at the Walnutport Community Church had a great love and respect for your father, and it's obvious that they care about you as well."

"I. . .I appreciate everyone's concern, but I'll be fine."

"You're in the valley right now, Betsy." His tone was comforting. "When we're walking through the valley, we must learn to reach out to God and His people."

She gazed into his dark blue eyes, so full of compassion,

WANDA E. BRUNSTETTER

and swallowed around the lump in her throat. "Thank you for that reminder, Pastor William. I've said the same thing to others I've ministered to through the Salvation Army, but it's much harder to accept help than it is to give it."

"I know." He took her hand, and his warm fingers wrapped around hers in a gentle squeeze. "Never be afraid to ask any of us for help. And if ever you need to talk, I'm willing to listen."

Chapter 18

———✳———

A steady *tap*, *tap*, *tap* roused Betsy from her slumber. She yawned, stretched, and pulled herself to a sitting position. She'd curled up on the sofa shortly after breakfast and must have fallen asleep. It had been a week since Papa's death, and still she wasn't sleeping well, so an occasional catnap was probably good for her.

The tapping continued, and Betsy stumbled to the front door, unmindful of her wrinkled dress or tangled hair. When she opened the door, she discovered Kelly standing on the porch, holding a wicker basket.

"I hope I'm not interrupting anything, but I brought a hot meal for your lunch," Kelly said with a friendly smile.

Despite her best efforts, Betsy released a noisy yawn. "Thanks. I haven't felt like cooking much lately, and I've appreciated all the meals the ladies from church have brought in this week." Remembering her manners, she opened the door wider. "Won't you come in, Kelly?"

"You look as if you've been sleeping, and I don't want to disturb you. I can just leave the meal and be on my way."

Betsy pushed a wayward strand of hair out of her face and tried to smile. "That's okay. I was just dozing on the sofa, but I need to get some things done yet today." She stepped aside and motioned Kelly to follow her down the hall.

"Is there anything I can do to help?" Kelly asked when they entered the kitchen. She placed the basket on the table and took a seat.

"Don't you have things to do at the store?"

"Mike said he could manage while I came to see you."

"What about your children? Who's watching them?"

"They're visiting my sister and her family today, so I'd be pleased to stay awhile if you need help with anything."

Betsy paced the length of the kitchen floor, feeling frustrated and kind of jittery. "I guess you could help me pack."

Kelly's eyebrows lifted in obvious surprise. "Pack? Are you going somewhere?"

Betsy stopped pacing and leaned against the counter. "I suppose I'll return to New York. Now that's Papa's gone, there's really no reason for me to stay here."

"Yes there is." Kelly stood and moved over to stand beside Betsy. "Our church needs you—I need you."

Tears welled in Betsy's eyes, blurring her vision. She used to see Kelly as her rival, but since she'd returned to Walnutport, they'd become friends. "That's nice to hear," she murmured. "But the church got along fine without me during the four years I lived in New York, and so did you."

Kelly gave Betsy a hug. "We didn't know what we were missing."

It felt good to be appreciated, and Betsy was about to comment when a knock sounded at the front door again. "Guess I'd better see who that is."

Kelly nodded. "I'll put the stew I brought on the stove so it stays warm."

"Thanks." Betsy hurried out of the room and down the hall. When she opened the door, she found Pastor William standing on the porch with his Bible tucked under his arm.

"Hello, Betsy," he said. "I missed seeing you in church Sunday morning, so I decided to check up on you today."

"I didn't feel up to coming to church, so I was glad Sarah Turner was willing to teach my Sunday school class."

A look of understanding flashed across his face. "It had only been a few days after your father's funeral, so I'm sure you weren't up to going anywhere yet."

Betsy nodded. The truth was, she still felt uncomfortable seeing people or trying to make idle conversation. She missed Papa terribly, and all she wanted to do was crawl into bed, pull the covers over her head, and sleep until the pain subsided.

"How are you doing today, Betsy?"

Instinctively she reached up to smooth the tangles in her hair, which she hadn't bothered to put up in a bun this morning. "I'm doing all right. Kelly Cooper's out in the kitchen, heating some stew she brought for lunch."

William shifted from one foot to the other. "Well, since you've already got company, I guess I should probably be on my way."

"Don't leave on my account," Kelly said as she stepped into the hallway. "There's more than enough stew for the three of us. So if you have the time, Betsy and I would be pleased to have you join us for lunch."

William sniffed the air and grinned. "It does smell good. Sure, I'd be happy to join you."

As William sat at the kitchen table with a bowl of stew and a plate of biscuits sitting before him, he glanced across the table at Betsy. Her face looked drawn, and her eyes were dark and hollow, as if she hadn't slept in several days. He figured she probably hadn't had a good night's rest since her father died. He grimaced. This was one area of the ministry where he fell seriously short. He'd always had trouble knowing what to say to someone who was grieving.

He glanced over at Kelly, who sat beside Betsy. "This is good stew. It's real flavorful."

She grinned back at him. "Thanks. It's one my mama used to make a lot when I was a girl leading Papa's mules up the towpath."

"That must have been hard work for a child."

"It was."

"Do you ever miss it?"

She shook her head. "I'm happy to spend my days raising our children and helping Mike at the store. When I have the time, I like to draw and paint pictures, too."

"Kelly's quite the artist," Betsy spoke up. "Mike even added a small art gallery onto their store so Kelly could paint and sell her artwork there." She smiled, although it never quite reached her eyes. "Several years ago I was the recipient of one of Kelly's beautiful charcoal drawings."

"It was just a silly old picture of two children fishing along the canal," Kelly said. "I'd given a couple of my pictures to Mike to sell in his store, and he ended up giving one of them to Betsy for her birthday."

William looked back at Betsy and noticed her flushed cheeks. It made him wonder if she and Mike had been boyfriend and girlfriend at one time.

"Papa invited Mike to dinner to celebrate my birthday one year." Betsy toyed with the handle of the spoon lying next to her half-eaten bowl of stew. "I think the poor man felt obligated to bring me a present."

WANDA E. BRUNSTETTER

"Betsy used to have her eye on Mike," Kelly said. "Then I came along and stole him away."

Betsy's blush deepened, and she stared at the table. "I was a terrible flirt back then, and I'd give anything if I could undo the past."

"It's okay," Kelly said, reaching over to pat Betsy's arm. "I might never have fallen for Mike if you hadn't made me feel so jealous."

"There was nothing to be jealous about. Mike only had eyes for you, and you're a much better wife for him than I could have been."

All this talk about love and marriage conjured up memories of the woman William had once loved and had almost married. Maybe Beatrice had done him a favor by breaking things off. Maybe she wouldn't have made a good preacher's wife.

"Did you know that Betsy's thinking of returning to New York?"

Shock spiraled through him as he turned to face Betsy. "You want to leave Walnutport?"

She shrugged. "I only came back to care for my father. Now that he's gone, there doesn't seem to be any reason for me to stay."

"That's not true. You're needed at church—as the organist and as a Sunday school teacher."

Betsy took a sip of water. "I'm sure you'll find someone to fill those positions after I'm gone."

"Does that mean you're definitely planning to leave?" He wondered how he could talk her out of going and why it mattered so much.

Betsy opened her mouth as if to reply, but Kelly cut her off. "I think she should pray about it, don't you, Pastor?"

He gave a quick nod. "I'll be praying, too."

Chapter 19

*A*s Betsy sat on the top porch step with Bristle Face in her lap, she reflected on her situation. Almost two weeks had passed since her father's death, and still she hadn't made a decision. If she went back to New York, she could continue with her work for the Salvation Army, which she knew would give a sense of purpose to her life. If she stayed in Walnutport, she could continue to play the organ for church and teach Sunday school, and both activities would help to further the Gospel.

"If I leave here, who's going to take care of you, little guy?" Betsy murmured as the terrier nuzzled her hand with his cold, wet nose. "You miss Papa, too, don't you, boy?"

The dog responded with a grunt, and she rubbed his silky ears. "I could see if Pastor William might be willing to take you, but there's the problem of his cranky housekeeper." Mrs. Bevens had never given any indication that she liked Bristle Face. She'd seemed quite upset when the dog kept running over to the parsonage before the fence was built, and she'd been adamant about Betsy keeping Bristle Face at home.

Betsy knew that if she stayed in Walnutport, she might lose her heart to a man who saw her as nothing more than a member of his congregation. And if she wasn't careful, she might end up throwing herself at him, or at least it could appear as if she was doing that.

She squeezed her eyes shut as the truth hit her full in the face. She didn't know when it had happened, but she had fallen in love with the new pastor. *Oh Lord, what would You have me to do? Should I move back to New York or stay here in Walnutport?*

"Yoo-hoo, Betsy! Can you hold on to your dog so I can come into the yard and speak with you about something important?"

Betsy's eyes snapped open, and she squinted against the glare of the afternoon sun. Freda Hanson stood on the walkway in front of the house, frantically waving her hand.

"Come on in. I'll put Bristle Face in the backyard." Betsy hoisted the terrier into her arms and hurried around back. When she returned, she found Freda sitting in one of the wicker chairs on the porch, so she took a seat in the other chair. "What did you wish to speak with me about?"

Freda leaned close to Betsy. "There's a rumor going around that you're thinking of leaving Walnutport. Is it true?"

Betsy nodded. "I've considered going back to New York and resuming my work with the Salvation Army."

"From the accounts I've read in the newspapers, the Salvation Army is a fine organization that does plenty of good deeds." Freda pursed her thin lips. "But you can serve the Lord here in this community, don't you think?"

Freda was the third person since Papa's death to suggest that Betsy was needed here. Could this be God's way of letting her know that He wanted her to stay? Wasn't it what she wanted, too?

"If you decide to stay, Ben and I will allow you to keep living in this house for as long as you like." Freda turned in her chair and motioned toward the front door.

"I know you only gave us the house to use because Papa was ill and had served as your pastor for so many years." A lump formed in Betsy's throat. "If I do stay on, I'll insist on paying you something for the rent."

"Does that mean you've decided to stay?"

"I suppose so. At least for now."

"That's wonderful, and there's no hurry about you paying any rent either. We can talk about that some other time." Freda reached over and clasped Betsy's hand. "Now, I must tell you about the box social our church ladies are planning for next Saturday. We're hoping you will take part in it."

Betsy shook her head. "I'm really not up to socializing yet."

"Oh, but this is for such a good cause. All the money that comes in during the bidding will go to our mission fund."

The words *mission fund* struck a chord with Betsy. How could she ignore something as important as that? At one time she had planned to serve in the mission field herself, and she knew missionaries who were sent to foreign countries needed all the funds they could get. "You can count on me to make a box lunch for the social, but I may not be there to see it bid on."

Freda frowned. "Not be there? Betsy, every woman who donates a box lunch should be in attendance that day. Please say you will come."

Betsy sat there a moment, mulling things over. Finally she released a sigh and nodded. "All right, I'll be at the box social."

The church basement was abuzz with activity, as everyone took a seat to await the bidding at the box social. Boxes and baskets in various sizes and shapes adorned the long wooden table at one end of the room, while the men who'd come to bid and the women who'd donated box lunches sat around the room in segregated groups. William had been asked to oversee this event, and though he'd hoped to act as the auctioneer, Freda Hanson insisted that her husband fill that role. She'd told William he needed a chance to bid on a lunch, and she'd sweetened the deal by letting him know that one of the lunch boxes included a piece of peach pie, which William had told Freda was his favorite kind.

As William took a seat beside Patrick O'Grady, the town's young, able-bodied blacksmith, he glanced across the room and noticed Betsy Nelson sitting beside Hortence Andrews. He was surprised to see Betsy, knowing she was still in mourning and hadn't attended church since her father's death. He'd heard through Freda that, for the time being, Betsy planned to remain in Walnutport, and that pleased him more than he cared to admit. He told himself he was just doing his pastoral duties by being attentive to her needs, but deep down he knew better.

When someone tapped William on the shoulder, he drew his gaze away from Betsy and turned. "Look for a white hatbox with a yellow ribbon, Pastor," Freda whispered in his ear. Before he could comment, she skirted across the room to join the married women.

Once again William focused on the colorful boxes sitting on the table. He spotted a white hatbox, but the ribbon tied around it was green, not yellow. His gaze went from one box to the next: a wicker basket with flowers tied to the handle; a short, square box covered with a red-and-white checkered cloth; a small silver bucket with two purple ribbons attached to the handle; a white hatbox with a bright yellow ribbon—that must be the one Freda spoke of—the one with the peach pie inside. *That's the one I'll bid on,* he decided.

Ben took his place behind the table and held up one hand to get everyone's attention. "The bidding's about to begin. We'll start with this one first." He held up a yellow basket.

William watched with interest as the bidding began. Various boxes went from fifty cents all the way up to three dollars. Since it was for a worthy cause, he was prepared to bid as much as five dollars for the box with the yellow ribbon.

When Ben got to the box William wanted, the auctioneer started the bidding at one dollar. Lars Olsen took the price up to two dollars. William quickly bid three, and from there the cost went to four. "We've got a four-dollar bid on this lovely hatbox!" Ben hollered. "Who'll give me five?"

William's hand shot up. He could almost taste the savory sweetness of that peach pie, and he licked his lips in anticipation.

"The bid's at five dollars. Now who'll give me six?"

The room became silent.

"Five, going once. Five, going twice." Ben slapped his hand on the table. "This lunch box has been sold to the preacher for five dollars!"

William stepped forward and picked up the hatbox,

bending down to sniff the lid. A delicious peach aroma tickled his nose, and he smiled with satisfaction. He hoped there were two pieces in there, because it would be hard to divvy up that peach pie with the woman who'd prepared the box lunch and with whom he knew he must share the meal.

Ben motioned to the women's side of the room. "Will the person who made the lunch inside the box our pastor just purchased please step forward?"

All heads turned, and William's mouth went dry when Betsy Nelson stood and walked slowly toward him.

Lars elbowed William in the ribs. "Sure hope she's got somethin' in that box worth five dollars."

Chapter 20

*B*etsy squirmed as she watched William spread a quilt on the grass behind the church, knowing they would be sharing a meal together. When she'd agreed to make a lunch for the box social, it hadn't occurred to her that the man who'd buy her lunch would turn out to be Pastor William.

"There, it's all ready. Won't you have a seat?" He nodded toward the quilt.

She smiled. At least she hoped it was a smile. Her knees knocked so badly and her face had heated up so much that she wasn't sure what her expression looked like.

Once they were seated on the quilt, Pastor William offered a blessing, and Betsy opened the hatbox lid. "I hope you like cold chicken," she said, chancing a peek at him.

"Has it been cooked?" he asked with a mischievous twinkle in his eye.

"Of course." She giggled and noticed that, for the first time all day, she felt relaxed. "The dill pickles and coleslaw are the only raw items in this meal."

"If I didn't know better, I'd think you had prepared this special lunch just for me."

"What do you mean?"

"Fried chicken, dill pickles, peach pie—all my favorites."

Betsy squinted, while pointing to the hatbox. "How did you know there's peach pie in there?"

A shadow crossed his face, and he quickly looked away. "Uh—a little birdie informed me."

"Freda Hanson is the only one I told that I'd made peach pie."

The pastor nodded. "Right before the bidding started, Freda whispered in my ear that the white hatbox with a yellow bow had peach pie in it." He glanced across the yard where Ben and Freda sat on a blanket, sharing the lunch Freda had prepared for them.

Betsy gritted her teeth.

Pastor William chuckled. "Oh well, at least I get to have my pie and eat it, too."

She smiled. It was nice to know the pastor had a sense of humor, and Betsy was overcome with the realization that this was the first time since Papa's death that she'd been able to find joy in something.

She reached inside the hatbox and removed the main course, a jug of cold tea, and two thick slices of peach pie for dessert. Then she took out plates, silverware, and a cup for each of them.

"If this tastes half as good as it looks, I'm in for a real treat," Pastor William said, reaching for a drumstick.

"Papa always said I was a good cook, almost as good as Mama used to be."

He bit into the chicken and smacked his lips. "I can't imagine anyone's chicken tasting better than this."

Betsy's neck heated up, and the warmth spread quickly to her cheeks. She wasn't used to getting such compliments—especially from such an attractive man. She felt something for Pastor William, no matter how hard she tried to deny it.

"I heard from the Hansons that you've decided to stay in Walnutport," he said, taking their conversation in another direction.

Betsy nodded. "For now, anyway."

"I'm glad to hear that."

She poured some tea and took a quick drink, hoping it might help calm her nerves. Was it possible that Pastor William wanted her to stay because he had feelings for her? No, that couldn't be. He was just being kind. He probably wanted her to stay so he wouldn't have to look for someone else to play the organ and teach the girls' Sunday school class.

Betsy dismissed her thoughts and decided to enjoy the meal as she listened to Pastor William talk about various needs in the church and how he was finally getting to know the people in his congregation.

They'd just begun clearing away their dishes when Kelly and Mike showed up. Mike suggested the pastor join him in checking on a broken window in the church that needed to be replaced.

Pastor William thanked Betsy for the delicious lunch and excused himself, then Kelly dropped to the quilt beside Betsy. "How did your lunch go?"

"Fine. How was yours?"

"It was good."

Betsy glanced around to be sure no one was listening. "I think Freda Hanson planned it so Pastor William would bid on my hatbox and end up having to eat lunch with me."

Kelly's eyebrows lifted. "Really? You think she's trying to get the two of you together?"

Betsy nodded. "From a couple of things Freda has said to me recently, I get the feeling that she thinks I would make a good pastor's wife."

"She's right. You would."

"I don't think so. I'm too outspoken, and besides, the pastor's not romantically interested in me."

"Then how come he seemed to be having such a good time over here this afternoon?"

"He was being kind and polite, like any good preacher

would be with someone from his congregation."

"Puh!" Kelly waved her hand, as though she were batting at a pesky fly. "If you can't see the way that man looks at you, then you'd better make an appointment with Dr. McGrath and ask him to check your eyes."

Betsy picked at a piece of lint on her dark blue skirt and remained silent. If Kelly wanted to think the preacher had eyes for her, that was Kelly's problem. Betsy was sure he'd only been acting polite today, and the kindness he'd shown toward her was no different than what he would have shown to any of his church members.

Kelly nudged Betsy's arm. "Changing the subject, I was wondering if you'd be free to have supper at our house next Friday."

At first Betsy was tempted to turn down the invitation, but then she thought about how much fun it would be to spend time with Kelly's two little ones. "I'd be happy to join you for supper next week," she said with a nod. "Is there anything I can bring?"

"Just a hearty appetite. Oh, and why don't you wear your hair down that night? It looks so pretty when it's hanging down your back."

Betsy didn't see what difference it made how she wore her hair when she went to the Coopers' house, but she agreeably nodded.

"Great." Kelly patted Betsy's hand. "It will be a fun evening, I'm sure."

Chapter 21

*I*t was nice of you to invite me to join you and your family for supper tonight,"Betsy said as she stepped into Kelly's cozy kitchen. It was a large room with blue- and white-checkered curtains hanging at the windows and a matching cloth draped over the wooden table. "I know how busy you are with the store and all, so I hope it wasn't too much trouble to fix this meal."

Kelly shook her head and moved over to the counter, where an abundance of fresh vegetables lay beside a huge wooden bowl. "Since our home is attached to the back of the store, it's easy for me to pop over here and get something going on the stove." She nodded toward the table. "Have a seat, and we can visit while I finish getting supper ready."

Betsy glanced around the room. "What needs to be done? I'd be happy to help in any way I can."

Kelly grabbed a head of lettuce and started tearing off the leaves then dropping them into the bowl. "The ham and potatoes are staying warm in the oven, and I just need to finish making the salad, so there's not much else to do right now."

Betsy was about to pull out a chair and sit down when a thought popped into her head. "What about the children? Do they need someone to keep them entertained until supper is ready?"

Kelly looked over her shoulder and grinned. "The little ones are in the living room with their papa, so I'm sure they're bein' well cared for." She nodded toward the cupboard across the room. "I guess you could set the table though."

Betsy pushed the chair in and hurried across the room, glad for the opportunity to do something useful.

When Kelly opened the oven door, the tantalizing aroma of baked ham floated into the room. It was at that moment that Betsy realized she hadn't eaten anything since breakfast, and even that had been a meager meal. Since Papa had died, she hadn't felt much like cooking. Besides, her appetite had diminished. But standing in this warm, welcoming kitchen with such a delicious smell teasing her nose, she realized hunger pangs gnawed at her insides.

Betsy reached into the cupboard and removed five plates.

She'd just begun to place them on the table when Kelly said, "Oh, I forgot to mention that you'll need to put out six place settings."

"Six? But there's only five of us—you, Mike, Anna, Marcus, and me."

"Pastor William will be joining us, too."

Betsy whirled around. "He—he will?"

"Uh-huh." Kelly closed the oven door and moved back to the counter; then she grabbed a tomato, sliced it, and added it to the bowl of lettuce.

"But I thought I was the only one you had invited. I didn't realize the pastor was coming, too." Betsy struggled with her swirling emotions as she leaned against the table. She had enjoyed spending time with Pastor William when they'd shared the box lunch last week, but it concerned her that some people from church had been trying to get her and the pastor together.

"You're okay with Pastor William coming, I hope. I mean, you like him, don't you?"

"What?" Betsy drew in a quick breath and fanned her face with her hand. The room had become so warm all of a sudden.

"Do you like Pastor William or not?"

"Of course I like him, but—"

"Mama, Marcus is botherin' me!" Anna shouted as she dashed into the kitchen from the other room. "Make him give my dolly back!"

"Where's your papa?" Kelly asked, reaching down to hug her fair-haired little girl. "Did you tell Papa that Marcus took your doll?"

Anna's lower lip jutted out. "I tried, but Papa's sleepin' on the sofa."

Kelly glanced at Betsy with an apologetic look. "Would you excuse me a minute so I can tend to this?"

Betsy nodded. "Of course."

Kelly wiped her hands on a towel, and she and Anna scurried out of the room.

Betsy moved back to the cupboard in order to get another plate. She followed that with glasses and silverware for everyone and had just finished setting the table when a knock sounded on the back door. "That's probably Pastor William. Oh I hope I look okay." She took a quick peek at herself in the oval looking glass hanging near the sink and hurried to the door.

When the door opened and William saw Betsy standing inside the Coopers' kitchen with her hair hanging around her shoulders in long, golden waves, his mouth went dry. He couldn't think of a thing to say, and all he could do was stand there, gaping at her.

"H–hello, Pastor William," she said, her voice quavering slightly.

"Betsy. I–I didn't expect to see you here," he stammered.

"Kelly invited me for supper, and only moments ago I found out she'd invited you, too."

He nodded slowly. Had he been set up? Was Kelly in on the little game that some of the other women from church had been playing while trying to match him up with a prospective wife?

"Come in," she said, stepping aside.

As a tantalizing aroma tickled his nose and made his stomach rumble, he shrugged his concerns aside and sniffed the air appreciatively. "Something smells good."

Betsy nodded and began to fill the glasses with water from a pitcher.

William glanced around the room, noting that he and Betsy were the only two people in the kitchen. Was Kelly planning for them to spend the evening alone? "Uh...where's the Cooper family hiding?"

"Kelly's in the living room, tending to a squabble between her two children."

"What about Mike?"

"Anna said her papa had fallen asleep on the sofa, so I guess Kelly will be waking him for supper, too."

"I see." William cleared his throat a couple of times. He didn't like the way he felt whenever he and Betsy were alone—all jittery and filled with a desire to be with her all the time. His heart, which he had vowed never to let love again, pounded away like the blacksmith's anvil every time Betsy was near. It made him wonder if he might be falling in love with her. He'd had those same feelings toward Beatrice. All that had left him with was a broken heart— and a determination never to fall in love again. Betsy seemed sincere and sweet, but he didn't know if she could be trusted. He'd trusted Beatrice, and what had that gotten him? He needed to hold on to what was left of his good sense, because Betsy was threatening to tear his defenses down.

"If you'd like to have a seat, I'm sure the Coopers will be joining us soon," Betsy said motioning to the chair nearest William.

He smiled despite the churning in his stomach and sat down.

"Have you chosen the songs for this Sunday yet?" Betsy asked, taking the chair opposite him.

He nodded. "They're all familiar hymns, so that's why I didn't bring you any music to practice this week." The truth was, he had purposely chosen those hymns so he wouldn't have to be alone with Betsy while they practiced the music. Each time they were together, he found himself wanting something he knew he couldn't have and didn't want. Or so he told himself.

"You're right. I probably don't need to practice the easier hymns." She smiled, and the dimple in her right cheek seemed to be winking at him.

William glanced at the door separating the Coopers' kitchen from their living room. *I wonder what's taking them so long?*

As if she could read his mind, Betsy pushed away from the table and stood. "Maybe I should let Kelly know you're here."

He nodded in reply.

Betsy had made it only halfway across the kitchen when the door flew open and the Cooper children zipped into the room. Anna held a rag doll in one hand and wore a smile that stretched from ear to ear. "I got my dolly back," she said, holding it up to Betsy. "And Marcus got a swat on his backside."

William stifled a chuckle as the two-year-old boy marched over to the table with a lift of his chin. Kids were sure cute. Too bad he would never have any of his own.

"Where's your mama?" Betsy asked, reaching out to touch one of Anna's golden curls.

"In there, tryin' to get Papa off the couch." The child pointed to the door then skipped across the room and climbed onto a chair. "I'm hungry."

Mike entered the room then, rubbing his eyes and yawning, and Kelly strolled in behind him. She smiled when she saw William. "I'm glad you could make it for supper, Pastor. Has Betsy been keeping you company?"

William's face heated. *I think I'm being set up. I'll bet Kelly stayed out in the living room just so Betsy and I could spend a few minutes alone.* He loosened the knot on his tie. *Well, it won't work. I will not give in to my feelings for Betsy Nelson, no matter how much I enjoy being with her.*

Chapter 22

*A*s Betsy stared out her kitchen window at the driving rain, her thoughts took her back to the supper she and Pastor William had shared at the Coopers' house two weeks ago. Despite her apprehension, the meal had turned out quite well. After they'd enjoyed some of Kelly's delicious apple pie for dessert, the children were put to bed, while the two couples spent the rest of the evening sitting around the kitchen table, drinking hot chocolate, playing dominoes, and visiting. Betsy had felt so comfortable with Pastor William that it had almost seemed as if she'd known him all her life.

"I wonder if he felt the same way about me," she

murmured. "He seemed much more at ease than he has in the past."

Bristle Face, who lay curled in a tight ball in front of the woodstove, lifted his head and whimpered, as if in response.

Ever since Papa's death, Betsy had found companionship and comfort in the dog. There were times when she wondered if Bristle Face actually felt her pain. Or maybe it was just that the dog missed Papa, too.

The window rattled from a rumble of thunder that shook the morning sky, and Betsy shuddered. She disliked storms, and this was one of the worst they'd had in quite some time. It had rained continuously for almost a week, and it didn't look as though it would let up anytime soon.

"Sure hope the canal walls hold together," she said with a shake of her head. If the canal was shut down, even for a short time, it would affect the boatmen, as well as everyone who lived or worked near the canal. It had happened several times during the years Betsy and her father had lived in Walnutport, but the community had always banded together and overcome even the worst of storms.

Another clap of thunder sounded, and Betsy moved away from the window. She had several shirts to mend for some of the canalers and figured she'd better get busy, since she had promised to have them done by tomorrow. She opened her mending basket, took a seat in the rocking chair by the woodstove, and set to work on one of the most tattered shirts.

Bristle Face lifted his head again and grunted.

"It's okay, boy. Go back to sleep. I'm just going to sit here awhile and sew."

The dog lowered his head and nestled his paws, but a sudden knock on the back door brought him quickly to his feet. He darted to the door, barking frantically, until Betsy shushed him.

She was surprised to discover Pastor William on the porch, wearing a heavy black jacket and a pair of dark trousers. It was the first time she'd seen him out of his suit, and his sopping wet clothes dripped water all over the porch.

"I just got the news that the canal has broken in several places," he panted. "Water's rushing everywhere, the towpath is completely covered, and already several homes have been flooded."

Betsy grimaced. "I'm sorry to hear that."

He nodded. "I know you don't have a lot of room here, but I was wondering if you might be able to put a few people up, should it become necessary."

"Of course," Betsy answered without hesitation. "I'm sure others in town will help, too. In the past when we've had a storm such as this, Papa opened the church for meals and lodging to accommodate those who had no other place to go."

"I've already discussed that idea with the board of deacons, and cots are being set up in the church basement as we speak."

"Would you like to come inside for a cup of hot tea?" Betsy asked. "I've got a fire going in the woodstove, and it will give you a chance to get dried off a bit before you head out into this nasty weather again."

Pastor William glanced over his shoulder. "I appreciate the offer, but I should probably get back to the church and help the men set up those cots."

Betsy nodded and was about to tell him good-bye when Bristle Face darted out the door and pawed at Pastor William's knees with an excited whine. "Get down, Bristle Face," she scolded. "You know better than to jump on anyone like that."

Pastor William bent down and patted the dog's head. "I think he misses his regular visits to the parsonage."

Betsy shook her head. "I believe it's you he misses. I've never seen Bristle Face take to anyone the way he has you."

He smiled and swiped at the raindrops that had dripped from his hair onto his chin. "Maybe I will take you up on that cup of tea. It'll give me and Bristle Face a chance to visit a few minutes."

"Right." Betsy opened the door farther and bid him entrance as a sense of disappointment flooded her soul. Why couldn't it be *her* Pastor William wanted to visit? Was she so unappealing that he would prefer a dog to her company? Well, she wouldn't flirt in order to get his attention—that much she knew.

"It's nice and warm in here," Pastor William said, stepping into the kitchen behind her. "I've never cared much for damp weather, and this drenching rain is enough to chill me clear to the bone."

"I know what you mean." Betsy motioned to the row of wall pegs near the door. "Why don't you hang up your jacket and take a seat at the table? I'll put a kettle of water on the stove and have a cup of tea ready in no time."

William did as she suggested, and as soon as he'd taken a seat, Bristle Face hopped into his lap. Before Betsy could holler at the dog, William smiled. "It's okay. I like the little fellow."

"That's fine, but he will have to get down once I put the tea and cookies on the table," she said with a shake of her head.

William's eyebrows lifted, and he wiggled them up and down. "Cookies? What kind have you got?"

"Oatmeal. I made a batch yesterday morning."

"I've never cared much for hot oatmeal as a breakfast food, but it's sure good in cookies."

Betsy smiled and hurried over to the stove. As soon as she put the water on to boil, she placed a tray of cookies on the table and took two cups down from the cupboard.

A short time later she joined him at the table, and

Bristle Face, who'd been put on the floor, lay under the table, snoring.

For the next half hour, Pastor William and Betsy discussed the storm, how they could offer aid to those who might be flooded out of their homes, and how good it was to know that many people from their church would be willing to help out.

Finally Pastor William pushed his chair away from the table and stood. "Thank you for the tea and cookies. I should get back to the church and see what I can do to help out. If things keep going as they are, probably several families will be in need of shelter by nightfall."

Betsy followed him across the room, where he slipped into his jacket and headed for the door. "As soon as I finish mending the shirts I promised to have done by the end of the day, I'll come over to the church and see what I can do to help."

He smiled and took a step toward her. "Thank you, Betsy. I appreciate that."

Betsy's mouth went dry. The strange sensation that came over her whenever Pastor William looked at her was unnerving. Even more unsettling was the urge she had to hurl herself into his arms and declare the love she felt for him. The old Betsy might have considered such a bold move, but now she would never dream of being so audacious.

"Maybe I'll see you a little later then." He turned and walked out the door.

❖

For the next several days, rain continued to pelt the earth. William spent every waking moment ministering to someone in need either at the church, where many had come to take refuge, or at homes where some who were ill were able to remain. When the rain finally stopped, a group of men began working on the breaks that had occurred in several places along the canal. Despite Mrs. Bevens's insistence that William's place was in town, he'd offered his assistance wherever he was needed at the canal.

As William settled himself at the kitchen table for his devotions one morning, he was overcome with a sense of gratitude and amazement as he reflected on how well the community had rallied to help one another during this unforeseen disaster.

He thought about Betsy Nelson and how each day she had spent several hours at the church, helping cook and serve meals for those who'd taken shelter there. At home, Betsy washed and mended clothes free of charge. She'd also taken Sarah Turner and her children into her home, because the first floor of their lock tender's house had been badly flooded. Since the boats weren't running and many of the locks were broken, including the one in Walnutport, Sarah's husband, Sam, spent his days helping with repairs on the canal breaks. At night, he slept on the one of the canalers' boats so he would be close at hand when the work began each morning.

Leaning back in his chair, William laced his fingers behind his head and closed his eyes. A vision of Betsy came to mind. He'd spent most of the night thinking about Betsy, in spite of trying not to. She seemed to be everything he wanted in a wife—if he was looking for one. She was talented, helpful, selfless, and kind. And she made some of the best-tasting oatmeal cookies he'd ever eaten.

"What's that silly grin you're wearing all about?" Mrs. Bevens placed a cup of coffee in front of him and tipped her head. "I would think as tired as you must be from working so hard this past week you'd be grumpier than an old bear."

His eyes snapped open, and he looked up at her sullen face. "On the contrary, I find helping others to be quite rewarding—even exhilarating."

"Humph! You'll wear yourself out if you're not careful, and I doubt your hard work will be appreciated."

He ran his fingers along the edge of his Bible. "Proverbs 19:22 says, 'The desire of a man is his kindness.' It's my desire to be kind and helpful to others because I care about them, not so they will show their appreciation."

Mrs. Bevens shrugged and moved over to the sink, and William went back to reading the Bible.

When a knock sounded on the back door, Mrs. Bevens hurried to answer it. She returned to the kitchen with Mike Cooper at her side. "I'm sorry to bother you, Pastor," he said, "but there's been an accident at the canal, and you're needed right away."

"An accident?" William jumped up, nearly knocking over his chair.

Mrs. Bevens pursed her lips. "Shouldn't the doctor be called for something like that?"

"Dr. McGrath has already been notified, and he's on his way." Mike's eyes were huge, and his lips compressed. "I'm thinking poor Sam Turner may have more need of a preacher right now than he does a doctor."

Chapter 23

William was relieved to see that Mike had brought along two horses. They would get them to the canal quicker than by taking the time to hitch up a wagon or trudging on foot through the murky floodwaters. After slipping his Bible into the saddlebag while offering up a prayer for Sam, he mounted his horse and followed Mike to the other side of town.

A short time later, they arrived at the Walnutport lock, which was where Mike said the accident had occurred. Dr. McGrath's rig was parked outside the lock tender's house, and several boatmen stood near the front door, wearing anxious expressions.

"The doc's got Sam inside on a table. Guess it's about

the only piece of furniture that ain't covered in water," Bill Bellini said, shaking his head. "It don't look good for Sam. No, it don't look good a'tall."

"Can you tell me exactly what happened?" William asked after he and Mike had dismounted and tied their horses to the hitching rail.

Bill nodded grimly. "A boat broke loose from where it was tied, and then it floated over to the lock and got jammed. Sam and several others were workin' hard at tryin' to get it free."

"That's right," another burly man spoke up. "Me, Slim, and Amos was tryin' to help Sam when things went sour." He grimaced and pulled his fingers through the ends of his wiry beard. "Sam was standin' on top of the lock, and his foot must have slipped, 'cause from what I could tell, he tumbled straight into the water. Next thing we knew, the boat shifted, and Sam was smashed between it and the lock." The boatman paused and gulped in a quick breath. "It took all three of us to get him out, but I ain't sure it did much good, 'cause that poor fellow's in real bad shape."

William reached into his saddlebag and pulled out his Bible before following Mike into the house. "May God's will be done," he whispered.

"Are you sure you wouldn't like another cup of tea?" Betsy asked Sarah as the two of them sat at her kitchen table, doing some mending while Sarah's three little ones took their naps.

Sarah looked up and smiled. "I've already had three cups, and if I have one more, I might float right out the door."

Betsy chuckled. She enjoyed Sarah's company and, during the time Sarah and the children had been staying with her, the two of them had gotten better acquainted. Betsy had come to realize that she and Sarah could be good friends, and she hoped they could spend more time together even after Sarah and her children were able to return home. *Of course,* she reasoned, *Sarah keeps awful busy caring for her little ones and helping Sam bring the canal boats through the lock. She probably doesn't have a lot of free time on her hands.*

A knock at the back door drove Betsy's musing aside, and she excused herself to answer it.

When she opened the door, she was surprised to see Pastor William standing there with a pained expression on his face. "Is. . .is Sarah here? I need to speak with her right away."

Betsy nodded. "Would you like to come in and join us for a cup of tea?"

He shook his head. "There's no time for tea."

Betsy grimaced. She had a sinking feeling that something terrible had happened and it involved Sarah's husband. "Please come in. You'll find Sarah in the kitchen."

Pastor William took a few steps forward and halted. He leaned close to Betsy's ear. "Sarah's going to need you at her side when she hears my news."

Not since the day Papa died had Betsy seen their pastor looking so glum, and with a sense of dread, she led the way to the kitchen.

Sarah looked up from her mending as soon as they entered the room and smiled. "Pastor William, it's nice to see you." Her smile quickly faded. "You look upset. Is something wrong?"

He moved quickly across the room and sat in the chair beside Sarah. Betsy took the seat on the other side of her. "There's been an accident at the lock." The pastor placed one hand on Sarah's shoulder.

"Is. . .is it Sam?" Sarah's lower lip quivered, and her eyes opened wide.

"Yes, Sarah."

"Wh–what happened?"

"One of the boats that had been tied near your home broke loose and got stuck in the lock. Sam and a couple of other men tried to get the boat out, and. . ." He paused and glanced over at Betsy as though seeking her help.

Betsy reached for Sarah's hand to offer support. She dreaded Pastor William's next words.

"There's no easy way to tell you this, but Sam—he fell into the water, and his body was smashed between the boat and the lock."

Sarah gasped and covered her mouth with her hand. "Is he. . .dead?"

He nodded soberly. "He died soon after I arrived."

The color drained from Sarah's face, and she slumped over. Betsy grabbed one arm, and Pastor William grabbed the other as they helped her over to the sofa in the living room.

Several minutes passed before Sarah was composed enough to speak again, and when she did, her first words came out in a squeak. "Was...was there time for you to pray with Sam?"

"Yes. I read him the twenty-third Psalm."

"Sam didn't always believe in God," Sarah said tearfully. "But two years ago he started attending the services Pastor Nelson held along the canal. One day he prayed and asked God to forgive his sins." Her voice broke on a sob. "He was a changed man after that and attended church nearly every Sunday."

Betsy was at a loss for words. All she could do was cling to her friend's hand and murmur, "I'm sorry, Sarah. I'm so sorry."

The next several weeks went by in a blur. Pastor William conducted the funeral for Sam Turner, helped finish up the canal repairs, and assisted Sarah and her family as they moved back to the lock tender's house. Betsy pleaded with Sarah not to go, insisting that she and the children could stay with her as long as they wanted. But Sarah was adamant about leaving. "I must support my children," she'd said over a cup of coffee one morning. "I'm responsible for the Walnutport lock now, and I've got to do whatever it takes to provide for my children's needs."

Betsy couldn't argue with that, but she did have some concerns about Sarah's ability to run the lock by herself. Sam's mother, Maria, who had been living in Easton with her older son since her husband's death two years ago, had agreed to move back to Walnutport to help care for Sarah's children. That relieved Betsy's mind some, and she was sure that many in the community would help the Turner family in any way they could.

Betsy had clothes to wash for some of the boatmen who were back to work hauling coal up and down the canal. Tomorrow morning she planned to go over to the church and practice some songs for Sunday morning's service. After that she hoped to visit Sarah and her children and take them a basket of food for their evening meal.

Reaching into the cupboard underneath the sink, Betsy retrieved a washtub and a bar of lye soap. Kelly had been trying to get her to buy some of the pure white floating soap they sold in their store, but Betsy preferred the homemade kind, believing it got the clothes cleaner. Besides, she had gone through a lot of soap since she'd started taking in washing, and the lye soap she made was cheaper than the store-bought kind.

She opened the back door and set the tub on the porch. Then she returned to the kitchen to get the kettle of water she had heated on the stove. Once that was dumped into the washtub and she'd added the bar of soap and stirred it around, she dropped three shirts in to let them soak. Then she went back inside to fetch her washboard.

When she returned a few minutes later, she was surprised to see Bart Jarmon, one of the canalers, standing on the porch. Bart was a tall, burly man with a thick crop of kinky black hair and a wooly beard that matched. As far as Betsy knew, Bart had never been married, and since he wasn't a churchgoer and had quite a foul mouth, it came as no surprise to her that he had no wife.

"I'm sorry, Bart," she said politely, "but your shirts won't be done until later today. When you dropped them off on Monday, I thought I told you they wouldn't be ready until late afternoon on Thursday."

He shuffled his boots across the wooden porch slats and grinned at her in a disconcerting way. "Figured I'd come by early, just in case."

Betsy motioned to the washtub on the other end of the porch. "As you can see, I've just begun my washing for the day."

Bart pulled his beefy fingers through the ends of his beard. "That's okay. I can wait."

Wait? Bart had to be joking. It would take Betsy awhile to get the shirts washed and rinsed, and then it would be a few more hours until they were sufficiently dried. When she told him that, he merely shrugged and plopped down on the top porch step with a grunt.

"Aren't you boating today?" Betsy asked, hoping the reminder of work might persuade the man to leave.

He shook his head. "Gotta hole in my boat that needs fixin', so I'm takin' a couple days off."

"Well then, shouldn't you be down at the canal, working on the boat?"

"Nope. Got Abe Wilson, my helper, doin' that."

"I see." Betsy shifted restlessly. Should she go about her washing and ignore Bart, or should she insist that he leave? Maybe it would be best to get on with the clothes washing. She moved to the other side of the porch, knelt in front of the washtub, and reached in to pick up the first shirt.

She'd only been scrubbing a few minutes when she felt a strong hand touch her shoulder. Turning, she was shocked to see Bart staring at her in a most peculiar way. "What's wrong? Why are you looking at me like that?"

His lips curved into a wide smile, revealing a set of badly stained teeth. "I was just wonderin' how come a purty lady like you ain't married."

Before Betsy could think of a sensible reply, Bart dropped to his knees beside her. "If you was my wife, you wouldn't have to wash for anyone but me, and I'd be the only one earnin' a living."

"I assure you, I'm getting along fine by myself." She

wrung out the first shirt, set it aside, and picked up the second one.

With no warning, Bart leaned closer, grabbed Betsy's cheeks between his calloused hands, and kissed her squarely on the mouth.

She jerked back, reeling from the shock of his kiss and feeling as though it was her mouth that needed a good washing instead of Bart's shirts. "How dare you take such liberties!" She plucked the rest of his shirts from the water, grabbed the one she'd set aside, and threw them at him.

As Betsy stood on shaky legs, she shook her finger in his face. "Don't come back here anymore, Bart Jarmon, because even if I were starving to death, I would never do business with you again!"

Chapter 24

*W*illiam placed his sermon notes on the pulpit and pulled his watch from the pocket of his trousers. He was supposed to meet Betsy here at ten o'clock so they could go over some songs for the service tomorrow; it was already ten fifteen, and she hadn't shown up.

Had she slept in this morning and been too tired to come? William smiled as he thought about how tirelessly Betsy had worked to help those who'd been without homes or jobs during the previous weeks of flooding. Betsy had shared her home, her food, and her time, and he'd never heard her complain.

He gripped the edge of the pulpit, as the truth slammed

into him with such force he feared he might topple over. He didn't know when or how it had happened, but he'd fallen hopelessly in love with Betsy. He'd foolishly lowered his defenses and allowed his heart to open up to this sweet, caring woman with the voice of an angel.

William whirled around to face the wooden cross that hung between the stained glass windows behind him then folded his hands and squeezed his eyes shut. *Heavenly Father, Betsy has given me no indication that she's anything like Beatrice, yet I'm afraid to trust again. I believe Betsy cares for me, but does she love me? Do I dare let her know how I feel and risk possible rejection? Oh Lord, please show me what to do.*

A door slammed shut, and when William heard the shuffle of feet, it ended his prayer. He turned and was surprised to see Ben Hanson enter the sanctuary, wearing a dour expression. Had something happened? Could there have been another accident on the canal?

He stepped off the platform and moved quickly toward the deacon. "What is it, Ben? You look upset."

The older man clenched his fists, as he held his body rigid. "I am upset, and I need your advice."

William motioned to the closest pew. "Let's have a seat, and you can tell me what's wrong."

Ben nodded as he sank to the pew. "Actually, it's my wife who's the most upset. And when Freda's upset, it upsets me."

William took the seat beside him. "What's the problem?"

Ben folded his arms. "Freda was heading over to see Betsy yesterday morning, and she was about to enter the backyard when she caught sight of Betsy kissing one of the canalers."

William's mouth dropped open, and a muscle on the side of his neck went into a spasm. Surely this couldn't be true. He couldn't imagine Betsy kissing any of the rugged boatmen who often used foul language and rarely came to church.

"I can see by your look of surprise that you're as shocked as I was to learn of this news." Ben slowly shook his head. "Kissing a man in broad daylight doesn't seem like something Betsy would do, but if Freda says she saw it, then it must be true."

William cleared his throat. "I'm sure there must be some logical explanation." *There has to be. Betsy can't be in love with someone else.*

"What kind of explanation could there be?"

"I don't know."

"Freda doesn't think we should continue to allow Betsy to rent our house if she's going to carry on like that with the boatmen."

William lifted his hand. "I can't believe you would evict Betsy when you haven't heard her side of the story. Besides, it's not our place to judge her. Only God has that right."

"I told Freda the same thing, but she says...." Ben paused

189

and clasped William's shoulder. "Will you speak with Betsy about this, Pastor?"

"I suppose I could." William stood, hoping Ben would take the hint and leave. If Betsy were to show up soon, he didn't think it would be good for Ben to be here when he confronted her about what Freda had seen.

"I think Freda was hoping it would be you Betsy would fall for, not one of the canalers like Bart, who's so rough around the edges." Ben shuffled his feet a couple of times and stared at the floor.

William grimaced as confusion swirled in his head like the raging canal floodwaters. If what Freda said she saw was true, then maybe the reason Betsy hadn't shown up at the church this morning was because she was too embarrassed by her actions to face the pastor.

"I'd best be getting back home to Freda. She'll be anxious to hear how my meeting went with you." Ben shuffled up the aisle, calling over his shoulder, "As soon as you've spoken to Betsy, let me know what she said!"

For the next several minutes William stood there, feeling too stunned and confused to know what to do. He needed to speak with Betsy, but how should he broach the subject of Freda's accusation? Should he simply march up to Betsy, tell her that Freda had seen her kissing one of the boatmen, and then demand an explanation? Or should he try to get Betsy to tell him what had happened yesterday morning of her own accord?

He pulled his pocket watch out of his trousers for the second time and noted that it was now ten thirty. She was obviously not coming. Maybe he should go over to her place and tell her that he was concerned because she hadn't shown up to practice the songs as they'd planned.

William started up the aisle and had just reached the foyer, when the front door opened. Betsy stepped inside, her cheeks flushed, and several strands of hair that had come loose from her bun were swirling around her neck.

"I'm sorry I'm late," she said with a huff. "I had a little problem with Bristle Face this morning, and it took me awhile to tend to the matter."

He felt immediate concern. "Bristle Face? What's happened to the dog?"

"It seems there was a skunk prowling around our house last night, and the dog must have gotten in its path." She shook her head. "I spent several hours trying to get that putrid smell out of Bristle Face's hair, but the poor animal still reeks, and I'm afraid he'll have to stay outside for a while."

William chuckled. He could just picture that little dog sitting in a tub of water, covered with lye soap and tomato juice.

"Shall we see about selecting some songs and practicing them now?" Betsy moved toward the sanctuary.

William halted, leaning against the doorjamb that separated the foyer from the sanctuary. "I. . .uh. . .need to discuss something with you first."

As Betsy followed Pastor William into the other room, a feeling of dread came over her. He looked so solemn, and the tone he had used when he'd said they needed to discuss something made her wonder if she'd done something wrong. Was he unhappy with the way she'd been playing the organ? She did tend to play a bit loudly, and maybe he thought the music was too lively.

When they reached the front of the sanctuary, he motioned to the first pew. "Please, have a seat."

She smoothed the wrinkles in her long, gray skirt and sat.

Pastor William took a seat on the same pew but left enough space between them to accommodate two people. He sat there several seconds, staring at his folded hands.

Unable to stand the suspense, Betsy turned to face him. "Is something wrong?"

His serious expression sent shivers up her spine. "It has come to my attention. . . ." He paused and cleared his throat. "Someone said that. . . ." He looked away as though unable to meet her gaze.

"If this is about my organ playing, I'll try to tone it down some."

"No, no, it's not about that. I. . .uh. . .someone said that they had seen you the other morning on your back porch with a man."

Betsy nodded. "I did laundry yesterday, and several of the boatmen came by in the afternoon to pick up their clean clothes."

He stood and moved to stand in front of the communion table. "It was one of the canalers this person saw you with, and you were. . .uh. . .kissing him."

Betsy's mouth felt so dry she could barely swallow. Someone must have witnessed what had happened between her and Bart.

"Is it true, Betsy? Were you kissing a man on your porch?"

Her face heated up. "Bart kissed me, but I did nothing to encourage it. I threw his wet shirts at him and said I never wanted to do business with him again."

At first, Pastor William looked relieved, but then he frowned. "If I wasn't a minister of God, I would march down to the canal, wait for Bart's boat to come through, climb aboard, and punch him in the nose."

Betsy swallowed around the laughter bubbling in her throat. Pastor William was jealous, and he wanted to defend her reputation. What a glorious thought! What a glorious day!

Chapter 25

*P*astor William continued to stare at Betsy in a most peculiar way, and a shiver started low on her spine and fluttered up her neck. "Are—are you upset because Bart kissed me?" she squeaked.

His ears turned pink, and the blush spread quickly to his cheeks. "I. . .I don't want to think about any man kissing you—unless it's me."

"Pastor William," Betsy murmured, feeling more flustered by the moment.

"I–I'm sorry. I shouldn't have said that. It's just that I. . ." His voice trailed off, and his gaze fell to the floor.

She left her seat and took a step forward. "You what?

What were you going to say?"

Slowly he lifted his head until their gazes locked. "As hard as I've fought against it, I find that I'm hopelessly in love with you, Betsy."

"You—you are?"

He nodded. "I was jilted at the altar about a year ago, and the pain and shame of it left me full of mistrust. I'd convinced myself that I could never love or trust another woman, but getting to know you has changed my mind."

Betsy swallowed hard and blinked against stinging tears that threatened to spill over. No matter what happened in the future, this special moment would be imprinted on her heart forever.

"I love you, too," she said in a voice barely above a whisper.

"What did you say?"

"I love you, too, Pastor William."

"I was hoping you would say that." He chuckled. "But don't you think it's time you started calling me William?"

She nodded slowly.

"You know what I think we should do?" he asked, reaching for her hand.

Her hand fit so well in his. It was as if they'd touched like this before, if only in her dreams. "What do you think we should do?"

"I think we should practice our songs for tomorrow and then go over to the Hansons' and have a little talk with Freda.

She needs to know the truth about what happened between you and Bart, so she doesn't spread any ugly rumors."

"I suppose that would be a good idea. And then I want to pay a call on Sarah and her children. I've made a big batch of pork float and thought I would take it there for supper."

He smacked his lips. "That sounds good. Maybe I'll accompany you there, and we can share the meal with them."

Betsy smiled. "I'm sure they would appreciate a visit from their pastor, and I would enjoy the company on the trip over there as well."

"That's good to hear, because the two of us have much to talk about."

As Betsy prepared for church the following morning, she burst out singing. " 'Praise God, from whom all blessings flow. Praise Him, all creatures here below. Praise Him above, ye heavenly host. Praise Father, Son, and Holy Ghost.'"

In all her thirty-one years, she had never felt so deliriously happy. She loved William, and he loved her. After a suitable time of courtship, he might ask her to marry him. Hearing his declaration of love had seemed too good to be true, and Betsy felt like pinching herself to be sure she wasn't dreaming.

"William is all I've ever wanted in a man," she murmured

to her reflection in the mirror. "He's kindhearted, gentle, handsome, even tempered, and next to Papa, he's the finest preacher I've ever heard."

Betsy reflected on how William had handled things when they'd gone to see Freda and Ben Hanson. He'd said there had been a misunderstanding and that what Freda had actually seen was Bart kissing Betsy, not the other way around. Betsy had then explained her reaction to Bart. Freda had expressed sorrow for jumping to conclusions and explained that she'd walked away after she'd seen them kissing, so she hadn't witnessed whatever had followed.

After Betsy and William had left the Hansons' home, they'd gone to Betsy's to get the pork float she'd made and then headed in Betsy's buckboard to the lock tender's house to see Sarah and her family. They had used that time to get better acquainted. When William had asked if he could court Betsy, they'd discussed various things they might do on a date. Since winter would arrive in a few months and the weather was turning colder, picnics were out of the question.

"But we can go for buggy rides, take long walks, and go out to supper at one of the restaurants in town," William had said as he held Betsy's hand.

"Come winter, we can go ice skating, sledding, or sleigh riding," Betsy had happily added.

By the time they'd reached Sarah's house, Betsy had been so excited she could hardly contain herself. She wanted to shout to her friend and to all the world that she and William were in love and that he'd asked to court her. But she'd held herself in check, knowing she could share the news with Sarah some other time when they were alone and she wouldn't embarrass William.

Betsy pinched her cheeks one more time, grabbed her shawl and Bible from the end of her bed, and hurried out of the room.

"You're going to do what?"

William pushed his chair away from the table and stood. He didn't care for the shrill tone of his housekeeper's voice, and he wasn't going to stay here and listen to one of her insistent lectures. "I'm going to court Betsy Nelson." He grabbed his Bible from the kitchen counter and started for the back door.

Mrs. Bevens jumped up and positioned herself between him and the door. "Where are you going?"

"To church, and I don't want to be late."

"But. . .but we need to talk about this."

"What's there to talk about?"

She planted her hands on her hips and scowled at him. "I can't believe you actually want to court that woman."

"Her name is Betsy, and I love her."

Mrs. Bevens's normally pale cheeks turned bright pink.

"She's not right for you, William."

"I think she is."

"There's been a conspiracy at church to get the two of you together, and I think Betsy is in on it. Why, I wouldn't be surprised if every encounter you've had with Betsy wasn't set up by her or one of her cohorts. I'm sure she's only after you for your money."

William bit back a chuckle. This conversation was bordering on ridiculous. "What money are you talking about, Mrs. Bevens? I'm a poor preacher now. Have you forgotten that?"

She shook her head. "Need I remind you that your family is quite well off. Some day when your father is gone, everything will be yours."

"I have a brother, in case you've forgotten. I'm sure my parents will see that Robert gets half of their estate after they've passed on." William grunted. "Besides, I'm sure Betsy isn't interested in riches or prestige, and when the time is right, I'm going to ask her to be my wife." Before Mrs. Bevins had the chance to comment, William rushed out the door.

Chapter 26

*B*etsy shivered against the cold as she stepped out the back door and placed Bristle Face's dish of food on the porch. It wouldn't be long until parts of the canal would have to be drained. Then all the boatmen would look for other jobs during the frigid winter months. Some would find work in the city of Easton, and others would stay near the canal to cut ice or find other jobs that would keep them busy until the spring thaw allowed them to boat again. Betsy wouldn't have as many customers to sew and wash clothes for, but she didn't mind. Hopefully she and William would be able to spend more time together, too.

Sunday after church, he had suggested that the two of

them have supper together on Friday evening. That was only a day away now, and she could hardly wait.

A blast of wind whipped against Betsy's skirt, and she pushed her thoughts aside. "Here, Bristle Face! Come get your breakfast!" she called, scanning the yard to see where the terrier might be.

When Betsy saw no sign of the little dog, she clapped her hands and called for him again. A few minutes later, the terrier stuck his head out of a bush where he had obviously been sleeping. He barked, dashed across the yard, leaped onto the porch, and skidded over to his bowl.

"Slow down," she said with a chuckle. "You can't be that hungry."

Betsy was tempted to stay and watch the dog eat, but the frigid wind drove her back to the warmth of her kitchen. Once inside she poured herself a cup of tea and was about to take a seat at the table, when she heard a knock at the front door. *I wonder who that could be.*

When Betsy opened the door, she was surprised to see Mrs. Bevens standing on the porch, wrapped in a heavy shawl and shivering badly. "I n–need to speak w–with you."

"Of course. Please come inside where it's warmer."

Mrs. Bevens nodded curtly and stepped into the hallway.

"If you'd like to go into the kitchen, we can have a cup of tea."

"That will be fine."

When they entered the cozy room, Mrs. Bevens took

a seat at the table and Betsy went to the cupboard to get another cup and saucer. She filled the cup with hot tea and placed it in front of Mrs. Bevens. "What brings you by on such a chilly morning?"

"I'm here about William."

Betsy smiled and slipped into the chair opposite the woman. "That was a fine sermon he preached on Sunday morning, wasn't it?"

Mrs. Bevens shrugged, then she picked up her cup and took a sip of tea. "I have known William for most of his life."

Betsy nodded. "I understand you used to be his nanny."

Mrs. Bevens squinted as her lips compressed. "I've been widowed for several years and never had any children of my own, but William is like a son to me." She paused and flicked her tongue across her lower lip. "So as his housekeeper and previous nanny, I feel it's my duty to care for him."

"I understand."

Mrs. Bevens shook her head. "No, I don't think you do. I don't believe you have any conception of what William needs or what makes him happy."

Betsy's face heated up. "I haven't known William nearly as long as you, but we are getting better acquainted, and—"

"I hope you have no designs on him because it wouldn't be right for William to marry someone beneath his social standing."

Betsy's mouth dropped open, and she set her cup down

so quickly that some of the tea spilled out and splashed onto the saucer.

Mrs. Bevens leaned forward slightly and stared hard at Betsy. "If and when William decides to take a wife, he will choose a woman who comes from the same background as himself. Someone like you, who lacks all the necessary social graces, would not make a good wife for the Reverend William Covington III." Mrs. Bevens drew in a deep breath and released it with a huff. "The only reason William has shown any interest in you is because he's become bored with this little hick town and needs some form of entertainment."

Betsy blinked as though coming out of a trance. She could hardly believe the things Mrs. Bevens had said to her. Surely they couldn't be true. The William she'd come to know and love couldn't possibly care about money, prestige, or social graces. "William doesn't seem bored," she said in his defense. "He's done well in his ministry here in Walnutport, and the way he reacts to those in his congregation seems genuine to me."

Mrs. Bevens took a long, slow drink of tea, and when she set her cup down again, her lips curved into a crooked smile. "I agreed to come here as William's housekeeper as a favor to his mother. She asked me to care for her son and keep an eye on him. She wanted to be sure that no one would ever hurt her boy again."

"You mean the way Beatrice did?" Betsy asked.

"You know about his fiancée?"

Betsy nodded. "I understand that she left him standing at the altar."

"That's right, and I'm here to see that it never happens again."

"I assure you, I'm not like Beatrice. I would never hurt William in such a way."

Mrs. Bevens pushed her chair away from the table and stood. "I plan to see that you never do."

Betsy stood, too. "What does that mean?"

"It means that if you do not stop seeing William, I will tell him that you're only interested in him because of his money and that you're looking for a way to climb the ladder of success by marrying into a prestigious family such as his."

"But that's not true." Betsy was close to tears, and she gripped the back of her chair tightly, hoping to keep her emotions in check. "I love William, and I think he knows me well enough to realize that I'm not after his family's money."

Mrs. Bevens tapped her toe against the hardwood floor. "There's something else you should know."

"What's that?"

"Even if William did choose to accept a commoner such as yourself, his family never could. Would you want to be the one responsible for coming between William and his parents?" She pursed her lips. "Don't make him choose between you and them. If you really love William, prove it by stepping aside so he can find someone who is worthy of being his wife. Someone he would not be ashamed to take home to meet his family. Someone his parents would readily accept."

Before Betsy could say anything more, Mrs. Bevens turned on her heel and marched out of the room. Betsy heard the front door slam shut. Resting her head on the table, she gave in to her tears.

———※———

When Betsy climbed out of bed the following morning, she had made a decision. She couldn't come between William and his family, no matter how much she loved him. The best thing for her to do was return to New York and her position with the Salvation Army, which she probably should have done right after her father died. If she'd left Walnutport sooner, she wouldn't have fallen in love with William and wouldn't be facing this problem.

Betsy's gaze came to rest on the Bible lying on the small table beside her bed. "I love William and would like to be his helper in the ministry," she murmured, thinking of how God had created Eve as Adam's helpmate. "But I will not come between the man I love and his family, so I have no choice but to remain an old maid and serve God without a husband."

She hurried to the desk across the room. Opening the top drawer, she removed a piece of paper and a pencil, then she took a seat in front of the desk. *I can't leave Walnutport without telling William good-bye.* Tears coursed down Betsy's cheeks, and she sniffed as she reached up to swipe them away. *I'll write him a note and leave it on the pulpit at church, for I could never say to his face all that's on my heart.*

Chapter 27

As William stepped into the church on Friday morning, he was overcome with a sense of joy. Tonight he and Betsy would be going on their first official date. He would escort her to the Walnutport Hotel dining room for supper, and tomorrow after they practiced some songs for Sunday, he hoped they could go for a buggy ride along the canal. Maybe by Christmas he would feel ready to ask Betsy to marry him.

Whistling one of his favorite hymns, William made his way to the front of the sanctuary and onto the platform. When he stepped up to the pulpit to place his sermon notes there, he was surprised to see an envelope with his name on it. He quickly tore it open and read the note inside.

Dear William,

After much prayer and consideration, I have come to realize that you and I are not meant to be together. I won't be going to dinner with you this evening, as there's no point in us beginning a courtship that could only end in disaster. I'm returning to New York and my job with the Salvation Army. By the time you read this note, I'll be gone.

You're a wonderful preacher, and the Walnutport Community Church is fortunate to have you as its pastor. I wish you well, and I pray that someday you'll fall in love with the right woman who might assist with your ministry in the proper way.

Most sincerely and with deep regret,

Betsy

William stood for several seconds, letting Betsy's words sink into his brain. *"Not meant to be together. . . Returning to New York. . ."* It made no sense. Betsy was nothing like Beatrice. Or was she?

"What a fool I've been to allow myself to fall in love again. I never should have trusted my heart—or Betsy Nelson. She was obviously toying with my affections."

William's hands shook as he crumpled the note and jammed it into his jacket pocket. *"You're a wonderful preacher. Walnutport Community Church is fortunate to have you."* He slammed his hand down on the pulpit, scattering his sermon notes to the floor. He bent to pick them up then slowly, deliberately ripped them in two.

"I'll never be able to preach this message on forgiveness," he said with a groan. "I may never be able to preach another sermon again."

He crammed the pieces that were left of his message into his other pocket, bolted off the platform, and rushed out of the church.

As he sprinted through the tall grass growing between the church and the parsonage, his thoughts ran amuck. *Why would Betsy say she loved me and then decide we can't be together? I'm sure it's not about money or prestige. Is she afraid I might ask her to marry me? Does she have reservations about being a pastor's wife?* He clenched his fists so tightly that his nails dug into his palms. *Dear God,* he prayed, *help me understand this. Show me what to do.*

Inside the parsonage William found Mrs. Bevens sitting in the living room with a piece of needlepoint in her hands. "William," she said, smiling up at him, "I thought you were going to the church to work on your sermon for Sunday."

He dropped into the chair across from her and let his head fall forward into his open palms. "I was, but something happened to change all that. I think I'll be getting out of the ministry altogether."

"Leaving this town behind is a good idea, but don't you think you should try to seek a pastoral position in another

209

church—one that has a larger congregation?"

He lifted his head and stared at her. "I don't care about having a larger congregation, Mrs. Bevens."

"But if you had more people attending your church, they could pay you more."

"I'm not worried about money either." He grimaced. "After reading the note I just found on the pulpit, I'm wondering if God might want me to leave the ministry."

"Note? What note?"

"From Betsy. She's left Walnutport and is going back to New York."

Mrs. Bevens released a noisy sigh. "That's good news."

"What did you say?"

"I said, 'That's good news.'"

"How can you say such a thing? I told you the other day that I'm in love with Betsy and had planned to ask her to marry me when the time was right."

Mrs. Bevens gave a quick nod. "And I said Betsy's not the woman for you."

William thought back to the conversation he'd had with Mrs. Bevens the other day, remembering how adamant she had been, saying Betsy was interested in his family's money and that she thought there had been a conspiracy at church to get the two of them together. Could she have expressed those things to Betsy? Might that be the reason for Betsy's change of heart?

He reached into his pocket and withdrew her crumpled

note, lifting it in the air. "Do you know anything about this, Mrs. Bevens?"

She pursed her lips and resumed her needlework. "How would I know anything about that note?"

"Have you spoken with Betsy lately?"

"We did have a brief conversation yesterday morning," Mrs. Bevens replied with a lift of her chin.

"What about?"

"Oh, just womanly things."

"What kind of *womanly* things?"

She released an undignified grunt and set her sewing aside. "If you must know, I spoke with her about your future."

"What about my future?"

"I told Betsy that she's not right for you and explained that your family would never accept someone as common as her."

"You did what?"

Mrs. Bevens tipped her head and looked at him like he was a little boy who'd done something wrong. "I was trying to protect you from getting hurt again—trying to keep you from making the biggest mistake of your life."

"Loving her is not a mistake." He stood. "Betsy is a sweet, caring, beautiful woman, and she would make any man a wonderful wife."

"Any of the boatmen or townsmen perhaps, but she's not right for you."

211

William paced between the fireplace and sofa. "How can you say that? How can you know what kind of woman I need?" He stopped pacing long enough to draw in a deep breath. "I love Betsy, and she loves me. At least that's what she told me before you stuck your nose in where it doesn't belong."

"I am only concerned for your welfare, William."

His head began to pound as the realization set in as to why Betsy had written the note. Mrs. Bevens had convinced her that she wasn't good enough for him and that his family would never accept her. It wasn't true—none of it. William didn't need a woman with a fine upbringing, and even if his parents chose not to welcome Betsy into their prestigious family circle, he didn't care. He loved her, and they were meant to be together. He was sure God had brought Betsy into his life, and he needed to bring her back, even if he had to travel all the way to New York, get down on his knees, and beg her to return to Walnutport.

Betsy had decided the best way to get out of town would be to flag down one of the canal boats heading to Easton and ask for a ride. That way she wouldn't have to worry about renting a carriage or asking someone to drive her there. So with her suitcase in one hand and Bristle Face's leash in the other hand, Betsy trudged determinedly toward the canal.

It obviously wouldn't work for her to take the dog along, but perhaps she could leave him with Sarah, whose children would probably enjoy having a dog of their own. She would miss the little fellow but was sure he would eventually adjust to his new surroundings. She would miss her friends in Walnutport, too—most of all, William.

As Betsy neared the lock tender's house, tears clouded her vision. *I was so sure things would work out for William and me, but maybe this is all for the best. He will go on with his life and find someone else to love, and I'll go back to my work at the Salvation Army.*

She'd found satisfaction in her duties there, but that had been before she met William. Even if she worked around the clock, she would never forget the love she felt for the special man she was leaving behind in Walnutport.

By the time Betsy reached Sarah's front door, she was so worked up she could barely speak. When Sarah's mother-in-law, Maria, answered her knock, it was all Betsy could do to ask for Sarah.

"She's in the kitchen, bakin' bread," Maria said, nodding in that direction. "Why don't you go in and surprise her?"

Betsy glanced down at Bristle Face. "Is there a place where I can tie the dog?"

"Bring him inside. He can play upstairs with the kids."

"Are you sure it's all right?"

"Is the critter housebroke?"

Betsy nodded.

"Then he's more than welcome to come in." Maria smiled and stepped aside.

Betsy set her suitcase inside the door and unhooked Bristle Face's leash. The dog let out a quick bark and darted up the stairs as though he knew exactly where the children were playing.

Maria went to the living room, and Betsy headed for the kitchen. She found Sarah bent over the stove.

"Hello, Sarah. How are you?"

Sarah closed the oven door and whirled around. "Betsy, this is a surprise. I didn't expect to see you today."

"I...uh...came to ask you a favor."

"What is it?"

"I'm moving back to New York, and I need a home for Bristle Face."

Sarah's eyebrows drew together. "You're leaving Walnutport?"

Betsy nodded.

"But why? I thought you liked it here. Walnutport's your home, and you've become an important part of our lives." Sarah took a step toward Betsy. "I was even hoping that you and Pastor William might—"

Betsy held up one hand. "There's no chance of anything happening between me and William."

Before Sarah could respond, a blaring horn sounded in the distance. "That's a conch shell blowing out there, so I must open the lock for the boat that's coming through."

Betsy grabbed her suitcase and hurried out the door behind Sarah, thinking this might be her chance to secure a ride. Sure enough, Amos McGregor's boat was lining up at the lock, and he was heading in the direction of Easton.

Betsy waited until the boat was safely through, then she rushed to the edge of the canal and called out to him. "Mr. McGregor, could you give me a ride to Easton?"

At first he tipped his head and looked at her strangely, but then he finally nodded. "Let me drop the gangplank for you, and you can come on board."

Betsy glanced over at Sarah, who had just closed the lock. "What about my dog? Will you keep Bristle Face?"

Sarah gave a quick nod. "Of course I will, but I really wish you weren't going."

A lump lodged in Betsy's throat, and she swallowed hard, trying to dislodge it. "It's better that I go. Better for everyone." She gave Sarah a hug, lifted the edge of her skirt, and hurried up the gangplank.

Amos hollered at his young mule driver to get the mules going again, and the boat moved forward. They'd only gone a short way when someone called Betsy's name. She shielded her eyes from the glaring sun and spotted William running down the towpath, waving his hands. "Stop the boat!"

Betsy looked over at Amos. "Please, keep going."

Amos nodded and signaled his mule driver to continue walking.

William cupped his hands around his mouth. "I need you

to stop the boat, Mr. McGregor! This is an emergency!"

Betsy's heart pounded so hard she could feel the rhythm of it inside her head. Why had William come here? Maybe it wasn't to try and stop her from going to New York. There could actually be an emergency. Perhaps something had happened to someone in Amos's family. "You'd better stop, Mr. McGregor," she said.

"Hold up them mules!" Amos shouted to his driver, then he dropped the gangplank.

William rushed on board and hurried over to Betsy. "I went by your place, and when I saw your buckboard, I figured you might have come down here, hoping to get a ride on one of the boats." He reached up to wipe the sweat from his brow. "Thank the Lord I'm not too late."

"Too late? Too late for what, Preacher?" Amos asked before Betsy could say a word.

"Too late to stop this woman from leaving." William picked up Betsy's suitcase and took hold of her hand.

"Wh–what are you doing?" she stammered.

"I'm taking you back to Walnutport where you belong."

She stared up at him as tears dribbled onto her cheeks. "Didn't you get my note?"

He nodded. "I also talked to my housekeeper, and I know about the things she told you yesterday."

"Then you must realize why I have to leave."

He leaned closer until his warm breath tickled her nose. "I love you, Betsy, and I don't give a wit about your station in life or my parents' money. If they accept you, I'll be happy and they'll be blessed, but if they choose not to accept you, then it's their loss."

"Oh William, I can't stand the thought of coming between you and your family."

"I don't think you have to worry about that. I'm sure once Mother and Father meet you they'll see how wonderful you are and will come to love you as much as I do." William grinned. "Well, maybe not quite that much." He dropped to one knee. "Betsy Nelson, I know we haven't had even one official date, but I've come to know you pretty well, and I think you would make a fine preacher's wife. So, after a suitable time of courtship, would you consider marrying me?"

Betsy stood with her mouth hanging open, too stunned to say a word.

Amos nudged her with his elbow. "I can't keep my boat stopped here all day, missy. Would ya answer the preacher's question so I can get on up to Easton with my load?"

Tears coursed down Betsy's cheeks as she smiled at William. "When the time is right, I would be most honored to become your wife."

Epilogue

Two months later

"You're the most beautiful bride I've ever laid eyes on," Kelly said as she brushed Betsy's long hair away from her face and secured it at the back of her head with a white satin bow.

Betsy smiled as she studied her reflection in the mirror they had set up in the classroom where she taught her Sunday school girls. She felt honored to be wearing the same satin gown William's mother had worn on her wedding day, so that was her "something borrowed." The pearls that graced Betsy's neck were brand new—a wedding present from her handsome groom. And for "something blue," she had chosen to carry a lacy white handkerchief with her father's initials,

HN, embroidered in blue thread. The hankie had belonged to her mother, so even though neither of Betsy's parents could share in this special day, it gave her a sense of comfort to know she carried something that reminded her of them both.

"I can hardly believe this is happening," Betsy murmured. "I feel like a princess from a fairy tale."

Kelly gave Betsy a hug. "You deserve to be happy, and I'm glad you didn't make William wait until next Christmas to make you his bride."

"I'm almost thirty-two," Betsy said, puckering her lips. "I don't want to be old and gray before we start our family. So when William suggested we be married on Christmas Eve, I could hardly say no."

Sarah chuckled as she stepped into the room. "I heard that remark, and you're not old, Betsy Nelson, soon-to-be Mrs. William Covington III."

Betsy reached one hand out to Sarah and the other one to Kelly, her two dearest friends. "William and I love each other so much, and neither of us could stand the thought of waiting a whole year to be married."

"It's wonderful that William's family could be here for the wedding," Kelly said, giving Betsy's hand a gentle squeeze.

Betsy nodded. "And to think I was worried that they might not accept me."

Sarah squeezed Betsy's other hand. "The real miracle is that Mrs. Bevens has found a personal relationship with the

Lord and no longer objects to the wedding." She wiggled her eyebrows. "Since William's housekeeper will soon be out of a job, I have to wonder if she might not end up marrying Rev. Carter from Parryville, who became a widower last year."

"That's right," Kelly agreed. "I saw Mrs. Bevens in the sanctuary earlier, putting the finishing touches on the decorations, and I couldn't help but notice the glances she and Rev. Carter kept exchanging."

"No one could be any happier than I am on this special Christmas Eve," Betsy murmured with a dreamy sigh. She took one last look at herself in the mirror and then turned toward the door. "Shall we go, ladies? I don't want to keep my groom waiting."

As Betsy walked down the aisle behind her friends, her throat constricted. The sanctuary was beautiful with glowing candlelight, boughs of holly mixed with evergreens, and red velvet bows decorating each pew.

Her gaze came to rest on William, looking ever so handsome as he stood at the front of the church beside his brother, Richard, and Mike Cooper. He was dressed in a black suit with a red bow tie, and he gazed at Betsy as though she were the most beautiful woman in the world. She felt blessed, and her heart swelled with joy. *Oh, I wish Papa and Mama were here to share this special moment with us.*

William's aunt Clara, who had volunteered to play the organ, switched from the traditional bridal march to the soft strains of "The First Noel." Betsy smiled through a film of tears. *That was Papa's favorite Christmas carol. Maybe he and Mama are looking down from heaven right now and can see how happy I am.*

"I love you, Papa," Betsy whispered. She stepped up to her groom and took hold of his hand. "I'm so glad I returned to Walnutport so I could meet you, Pastor William."

RECIPE FOR BETSY'S PORK FLOAT

Hunk of salt pork
2 large onions, cut up
6 large potatoes, diced
1 (14.5 ounce) can diced tomatoes
1 (14.5 ounce) can crushed corn
Biscuit dough

Cut salt pork into small pieces and fry in a pan to get the grease out. Brown and set aside. Fry onions in pork fat. Set aside. In large pot, combine potatoes, tomatoes, and crushed corn. Cook until potatoes are tender. Add the browned salt pork and onion; season with salt and pepper to taste. Bring to a boil. Make dough as you would for biscuits, and spoon into the pork stew to make dumplings. Keep covered and boil slowly for about 10 minutes or until dumplings are done.

About the Author

WANDA E. BRUNSTETTER is a bestselling author who enjoys writing historical, as well as Amish-themed novels. Wanda's interest in the Lehigh Canal began when she married her husband, Richard, who grew up in Pennsylvania, near the canal. Wanda and Richard have made numerous trips to Pennsylvania, where they have several friends and relatives. They've walked the towpath, ridden on a canal boat, and toured the lock tender's house. Wanda hopes her readers will enjoy this historical series as much as she enjoyed researching and writing it.

Wanda and her husband have two grown children and six grandchildren. In her spare time, Wanda enjoys photography, ventriloquism, gardening, reading, stamping, and having fun with her family.

In addition to her novels, Wanda has written two Amish cookbooks, an Amish devotional, several Amish children's books, as well as numerous novellas, stories, articles, poems, and puppet scripts.

Visit Wanda's Web site at www.wandabrunstetter.com and feel free to e-mail her at wanda@wandabrunstetter.com.

Other Books by Wanda E. Brunstetter:

Indiana Cousins Series
A Cousin's Promise
A Cousin's Prayer
A Cousin's Challenge

Brides of Lehigh Canal Series
Kelly's Chance

Daughters of Lancaster County Series
The Storekeeper's Daughter
The Quilter's Daughter
The Bishop's Daughter

Brides of Lancaster County Series
A Merry Heart
Looking for a Miracle
Plain and Fancy
The Hope Chest

Sisters of Holmes County Series
A Sister's Secret
A Sister's Test
A Sister's Hope

Brides of Webster County Series
Going Home
On Her Own
Dear to Me
Allison's Journey

White Christmas Pie

Nonfiction
The Simple Life
Wanda E. Brunstetter's Amish Friends Cookbook
Wanda E. Brunstetter's Amish Friends Cookbook, Vol. 2

Children's Books
Rachel Yoder—Always Trouble Somewhere Series (8 books)

The Wisdom of Solomon